ALWAYS YOU

MISSY JOHNSON

Copyright © 2013 Missy Johnson

All rights reserved

No part of this book may be reproduced in any form or by any electronic or mechanical means including information storage and retrieval systems, without permission in writing from the author. The only exception is by a reviewer, who may quote short excerpts in a review.

This book is a work of fiction. Names, characters, places and incidents either are products of the author's imagination or are used fictitiously. Any resemblance to actual persons, living or dead, events, or locales is entirely coincidental.

ISBN 9781496078995

First Printing: November 2013

BJJ Publishing

Always You

By Missy Johnson

Other books by Missy Johnson

Seduce (Beautiful Rose #0.5)
Beautiful Rose (#1)
Tease
So Many Reasons Why
Incredible Beauty
Inseparable
Desire

Coming soon:
Promiscuous
Provoke
Captivating (Beautiful Rose #2)

Connect with Missy

Twitter: @MissycJohnson
Email: missycjohnson@gmail.com
Facebook: www.facebook.com/MissycJohnson

Dedication

To my wonderful family

Prologue

Eleven years earlier...

"What are they talking about?" she asked, screwing up her nose.

I shrugged. "The same thing they always talk about," I said. "That I'm gonna get sick someday."

She scratched her head and her brow furrowed. "Well..." She paused. "We're all gonna get sick someday, right? So why do we need to worry about it now?"

I looked at the little girl. She couldn't have been more than seven years old with her long dark hair and sparkling green eyes. She was a child, but she had just spoken to me like no other person had.

"You wanna see my cubby house?" she asked suddenly. I nodded. She raced outside, me right behind her. We ran down the far end of the property, behind the garage, past rows and rows of homegrown vegetables. Eventually, a tiny shack came into view. We slowed to a walk as we approached the door.

Inside, everything was pink: the walls, the thick shaggy carpet—even the two small armchairs that sat in the middle of the room were a sickly bright pink. She stood smiling proudly, waiting for my reaction.

"It's very . . . pink," I commented awkwardly.

"I like pink," she said defensively, grabbing a doll and sitting in one of the armchairs.

I sniggered and sat down in the other. I was too tall for it, but I squished myself into it anyway.

"So, what's wrong with you?" she asked.

"I might have the disease my father has," I replied quietly.

She looked surprised. "So you don't even know if you're sick?"

I shook my head.

"Then why are you worrying about something that might not happen?"

I shrugged. I didn't have an answer for her. I worried because my parents did. I worried because I saw how much my father struggled. I worried because every day he was one day closer to death, and living the life I might be destined to live.

"It's hard to explain."

What I meant was it was hard to explain to a seven-year-old, who couldn't grasp the concept of life and death. At twelve, I'd lost my childhood. My life had revolved around this disease that may or may not one day consume me. The disease that was slowly killing my dad.

"I just don't get why you would worry about maybe getting sick, especially when it wouldn't happen for ages. You can't change it, so what good is worrying going to do?" She shrugged and picked at her doll's hair.

She said it so simply, like it was the most natural thing in the world. She'd pointed out something so obvious that I hadn't ever considered it before. Not really.

With all the years of paranoia, and grieving the loss of my life that may or may not happen in twenty or even forty years' time, my parents had never thought to allow me to actually live. I'd never had the freedom—or the desire—to explore my life.

The fact that it might be cut short should have been more reason for me to be living my dreams, not an excuse to hide away from everything I wanted. In the space of a few short minutes, this little girl and her simple outlook on life had changed my whole perspective on living and dying.

I should've known it was her when I saw her again on that first day of school. It should've been obvious. But she'd changed, and so had I. The years had changed me.

And I was soon to find out that they had changed her, too.

This is our story.

Chapter One

Wrenn

"What lies behind us and what lies before us are tiny matters compared to what lies within us." —Henry Stanley Haskins.

This time last year, I was normal.

I had a great life in Washington, D.C. We lived in a huge house with a big, sprawling lawn. I went to a school I loved where I had lots of friends. This time last year I had a mom and a dad. A brother who, although at times he bugged the shit out of me, I adored. Then, just like that, they were gone.

Dead. And I was alone.

They say things happen for a reason, but for the life of me, I can't figure out the reasoning behind that. What lesson could have possibly been big enough to require that kind of plan? To lose one family member is tragic, but to lose all three at one time is something I'll never get over. No matter how much time passes, nothing will fill that gap. That aching in my heart will never dull, as long as I'm alive and breathing.

My aunt and uncle have been wonderful. I have no idea how I would've gotten through the past year without their love and support. They took me into their home, no questions asked, trying their best to make me a part of their family. But I'll never completely fit in. As much as I know they love me, nothing can replace my parents and my brother.

All I can do is try to move on with my life and be someone my family would have been proud of. Try not to forget the wonderful things they instilled in me as a person.

I so badly want to make them proud of me. I can't bring them back. I can't erase the past, but I can control my future.

Chapter Two

Wrenn

Gasping for breath, I sat bolt upright in bed. Another nightmare. This time I'd woken up just as the car was careering into the tree, the moment of impact broken by my body jolting awake. The screams of Mom still rang in my ears as I tried to calm my body down. I shivered, the chill in the air colliding with the layer of sweat that covered me as I glanced at the clock.

Almost seven. No point going back to sleep when I had to be up soon anyway.

Wandering downstairs, I wrapped the tie of my light pink robe tightly around my waist. The accident was still so real in my mind, even after almost a year. Every little detail was so vivid, like it'd happened only yesterday. The sound of the tires skidding; the metallic taste of blood on my tongue.

And the crying. Oh God, the crying.

I rounded the bottom of the staircase and entered the kitchen. Layna was already up and making coffee, which shouldn't have surprised me. She slept less than I did. She raised her eyebrows, her brown eyes brimming with concern as she slowly stirred her drink.

"Up early," she commented, raising her eyebrows.

I nodded, focusing on her white robe, with little pink flowers embroidered around the collar. "Yeah. Another nightmare." I grabbed a cup and slid it down the black and white speckled marble counter to her.

She filled it and pushed it back. "Maybe talking to someone again might help?" she suggested.

I shrugged. Talking didn't help me sleep. Most nights I was lucky enough to get four broken hours, and I could function on that.

"I'll be fine. So, you've got the whole school in a twist with this new teacher you've hired. What's he like?" I asked, making the most of being related to the headmistress, and also changing the subject.

"Is it really that big a deal? He's only here for eight weeks. So long as he can control you all, that's all I care about," she joked with a laugh.

"How old is he?" I asked, raking my fingers through my long dark hair and twirling it into a braid over my shoulder. Like every other girl in school, I was hoping for young and hot.

"I'm not having this conversation with you, Wrenn. You girls are ruthless." She shook her head, her short blonde hair waving around her shoulders. I giggled and grabbed a granola bar, taking that and my coffee back upstairs to get ready.

Showered and dressed in my uniform—complete with black tights, considering it was freaking freezing outside—I went back downstairs and grabbed my backpack. It was just after eight thirty. With less than fifteen minutes until my first class, I made my way across campus. First up was History, and like every other student in the entire school, I was curious to see the replacement for Ms. Lucas. Rumor had it he was young and cute, and *that* had me excited. A cute teacher to fantasize over? Um, yes please!

Can you tell I didn't get out much?

Kassia was waiting for me outside the classroom when I arrived. She smiled when she spotted me. She was my best, and only, friend in this place. We'd started hanging out mainly because we were both social outcasts. Me, because I was…well, *me,* and her because she was a lesbian. Seriously, who outcasts someone just because they're gay? She was the one person in this place who I could actually have fun with. Without her, this place would have ruined me a long time ago. I'd learned quickly that personality didn't matter for shit in this place; all that mattered was your social standing and how much money you had. I was pretty damn low on both counts.

"Did you see Paige Warner today? I swear her skirt is so short I can see her twat," she mumbled under her breath.

I snorted.

"Ten bucks says she drops something in front of 'Mr. New-and-Apparently-Hot Teacher' just so she has to pick it up and give him a show. I wouldn't put it past her to give him a freaking lap dance."

"And you'll be right there watching," I smirked, nudging her in the side.

Paige was the definition of *skank* and the leader of the bitchy group that had taken it upon themselves to make mine and Kass's life hell. At least I'd only had to suffer through the past semester. Poor Kass had been putting up with this shit for five years.

Still, Paige was (as Kass would say) *Playboy Playmate* kind of hot, and like I could appreciate how sexy Roger Federer was—or maybe even this new hot teacher, Kass insisted on doing the same with Paige. She said that Paige's nasty personality meant she didn't have to feel bad about objectifying her, which always made me giggle.

We walked inside and took the only two seats available, right down the back. I snorted. Paige turned around and glared at me, her eyes reducing to narrow slits. I rolled my eyes. There was a law against me snorting now?

I'm sorry, but it was freaking hysterical that in the presence of a potentially hot new teacher, the whole classroom landscape had changed. The cool girls now sat front row center, chests stuck out, shirts unbuttoned, and legs crossed, ready to launch an attack on the poor, unsuspecting guy. I was already feeling sorry for him. Kass glanced at me and shook her head while giving Paige the finger. That made me snort again.

Sliding into my seat, I dumped my bag on my desk and began to unpack my books. *Uh-oh Mr. Teacher, you're three minutes late. Not a good first impression.* I flicked through my notebook, waiting impatiently for the class to begin.

Everyone sat anxiously, eyes on the door, waiting for it to swing open. When it finally did, it was so quiet I swear you could have heard a pin drop.

Holy mother of God.

This was our new teacher? My heart was racing just looking at him. He was fucking adorable.

He had light brown messy hair cut short enough that all he probably did was run a hand through it in the morning, and a crooked smile that sent my stomach into a spin. He was tall, athletic, and oh so sexy.

But what I noticed first were his eyes.

They were the deepest blue I'd ever seen. Beautiful long dark lashes framed them, and you couldn't help but be drawn in. I couldn't put my finger on exactly what it was, but there was something about him: something that made me lose all sense of everything else around me.

He looked about mid-twentyish, his tanned skin criminal in the middle of this harsh winter. I glanced down at my own pasty white skin and silently cursed him.

What the hell were they thinking, putting this poor guy in here among several hundred teenage girls, some of whom had been cooped up here so long that the only male specimen they had seen was the middle-aged science teacher with a beer gut that rivaled the belly of a heavily pregnant woman?

That was just *asking* for trouble, and trust me—no one could quite cause trouble like some of these girls.

He smiled again. Was he nervous? I sure would be. He looked pretty relaxed though, considering what he'd just walked into. He was like a piece of bloody meat in a tank full of sharks. I watched as he sat casually on the edge of his desk, hands in pockets, glancing around the room, apparently not fazed by every set of eyes in the area focused squarely on him.

"Hey, I'm Mr. Reid. Your teacher has gone into labor, I hear, so you're stuck with me for the next eight weeks."

God, even his voice was amazing—low and husky; he could've done voiceovers for porn ads. He smiled again and I nearly fell off my chair. Kass sniggered next to me. I shot her a look.

"A little bit about me. I'm fresh out of college, and this is my first teaching assignment. I'm originally from a small town just north of Los Angeles. I like good music and classic movies, and teaching is all I've ever wanted to do." He stood up and paced back and forth along the front of the room.

"How about I get to know some of you?" There was a low rumble of giggles, from myself included, everyone thinking just how much they'd like to get to know Mr. Reid. "So I want each of you to stand up, tell me something about yourself, and then ask me something. Sound good?"

We went around the room, girls nervously telling him something about themselves and then asking him a question, like his favorite color, or food. He pointed at Paige. She stood up, her eyes narrowing in on him as she smiled.

"I'm Paige, and I love dancing. I have a very flexible body," she practically purred. I groaned, embarrassed for her. Why didn't she just try and mount him then and there?

"Uh, well that's good for your dancing," he said, flustered. "And you're question for me, Paige?"

"Your phone number?" Everyone giggled. Kass caught my attention and rolled her eyes at me.

"Yeah, that's not going to happen." He chuckled, turning to Deena who sat next to Paige.

My heart began to pound as it neared my turn. What did I tell him? What should I ask? These seemed like the most important decisions of my life right now. Forget about college, and things that were actually important, all I wanted to was to stand out from the rest of these girls.

"And you?" His eyes met mine and I froze. Kass nudged me with her foot, forcing me back to reality. I stood up, my chair shooting back into the wall. I was the last person.

"I'm Wrenn. I-I'm originally from Washington, and I just moved here a few months ago." He smiled at me, his mesmerizing eyes making me dizzy.

"What do you want to ask me, Wrenn?" Hearing him say my name made me begin to sweat. I could feel the trickle of perspiration running down the back of my neck. I hated being the center of attention, but being the focus of *his* attention was almost unbearable. I said the first thing that came to mind.

"Mornings or evenings?" He raised his eyebrows at me, a shadow of a smile on his lips. "Are you a morning person, or a night owl?" I said, feeling the need to explain.

"Definitely not a morning person. I don't function very well before midday."

He grinned as I sank into my chair, his eyes lingering on me for another moment, before snapping back to attention.

"Well, let's get straight into things, huh? If you could all turn to page forty-six, one of you can run over what you covered in your last lesson."

I forced my attention away from the new teacher and focused on my books. I didn't need a distraction right now, no matter how sexy the distraction was.

The last year had been hard, and the last eight months had been hell. School was something I hated with a passion. It hadn't always been that way though. Last year it had been a complete and utter different story. That's how much things had changed.

Last year I had friends, a boyfriend, and a family.

And I wasn't surrounded by money-obsessed skanks all day.

Prep school was like my worst nightmare come true. When the thought 'I wish I'd died along with the rest of my family' crosses your mind on a daily basis, it's pretty obvious you're not in a great place emotionally. This place was hell. No, it was worse than hell, and I couldn't wait to leave. I was counting the days until I graduated.

Next month would mark exactly one year since I lost my family. It did get easier, but it's not something you get over. The nightmares came most nights, and were almost expected. It was like a constant recount of what I'd lost.

Every dream was the same: Me, in the back with my brother. I was wearing my new jeans. He had spilled soda in my lap and I was yelling at him. Mom was yelling at me to stop yelling, and Dad was trying to calm Mom down. I actually felt the moment the car hit the tree, the impact nearly splitting the car in half. I'd blacked out, and woken up in hospital.

I knew before they'd even told me that my family was gone. I can't explain it, but there was emptiness inside that hospital room, and I just knew. Maybe it was just anxiety I was feeling, but the dread I felt moments before they told me was inconceivable and unlike anything I'd ever experienced before. Unless you've lost someone close to you, understanding the pain of losing someone you love is something you'll never quite understand. I'd lost grandparents when I was younger, and though that was sad I'd moved on, because that's what you do. Death had always been something that was scary, but distant. I mean, nobody in my immediate family was going anywhere anytime soon, right?

You always think it will never happen to you. I used to watch the news and see these horrific events and feel bad for the people involved, but never really consider that it was something that could happen to me.

Until it did. Until that *was* me.

How I survived, I have no idea. My injuries were minor compared to how bad they could have been: three broken ribs and a broken pelvis. I was in the hospital for three weeks, and then in a hotel for another four, with Layna staying with me until I'd recovered enough to move here. I couldn't go back home; the idea of facing years and years of memories was too much.

It was the psychological trauma that took the longest to get over—that I'm still getting over. The first few weeks after the accident, it didn't feel real. It was like I was locked in a nightmare, just waiting to wake up. Even at the funeral, I struggled to comprehend that they were gone. I buried three family members in one afternoon, and there was still a part of me expecting Mom to come in and kiss me goodnight. Or for Jordan to call, begging for a lift home. Or to have Dad yell at me for using his car without permission.

The moment I began to accept what had happened was in the fourth week, as we were packing up the house. I'd stumbled across some photos taken during the vacation we took to Hawaii the summer before. We all looked so damn happy, lazing around the pool without a care in the world. Back then, my biggest problem had been deciding which shoes to wear with my new black and red sundress.

I just lost it. I sat on my bedroom floor crying for hours, calling my voicemail over and over just so I could hear their voices once more. Even now, I still have those messages saved.

Sometimes all I needed to hear was my mom saying 'I love you' to remember I was lucky enough to have had them at all.

***

After the excitement of first period, the rest of the day paled in comparison. I saw Mr. Reid in the halls a few times. My palms would begin to sweat and my face would heat up, but he never even glanced at me. I was invisible and I liked it that way. I could look at him and fantasize from a distance without looking like a sex-starved maniac—like every other girl in school.

The truth was, boys had been the last thing on my mind since the accident. Mr. Reid was the first guy I'd actually let myself be attracted to. That scared me a little, but knowing it wouldn't go anywhere was comforting.

On the way home, I stopped to use the bathroom. I was about to leave the stall when the door opened. Fucking great: it was Paige and her buddies. I quietly sat down, not game enough to leave until they had.

"How hot is Mr. Reid? I'd let him fuck me any day of the week," giggled Paige. Her friends laughed and agreed he was hot, arguing over who would have the best chance with him.

"Have you seen my tits? Obviously I'm going to win. No guy can resist these."

I covered my mouth, smothering a laugh. That had to be Stacie. She was always going on about her breasts, which, in my opinion, weren't all that.

"Whatevs. You'll all be paying up when I win. And I'll be using that money to buy some sexy lingerie for when I fuck him," Paige retorted. They all laughed and left the bathroom.

What the hell was that about? Fumbling in my backpack for my phone, I texted Kass.

Held up in the bathroom. Bitches talking about a bet and Mr. Reid. Gossip?

Kass might be an outcast, but she knew everything that was going on in this place, and usually right after it happened. My phone beeped.

Lol yeah. Who is going to kiss him first. Puke. Winner gets close to a grand. Think I'll win? ;)

I sniggered and shoved my phone in my pocket. Only here would this happen. These girls were insane. Someone should really warn the poor guy. He really had no idea what he was in for.

Chapter Three

Dalton

I pulled the classroom door shut, trying to ignore the group of giggling girls standing to my left, staring at me. I was slowly getting used to the attention—being the only male teacher at this school under the age of fifty, it sort of came with the territory. They eventually moved off down the hall, but not before more whispering and giggling. I shook my head and locked the door.

"They have a pool, you know."

I turned around. She was leaning against the opposite wall, her head tilted to the side as she studied me with her deep green eyes. Her long dark hair hung in waves down her back. She looked familiar, but that wasn't surprising, considering she was probably in one of my classes.

"A pool?" I repeated, bemused.

"Yes. Like, a betting pool. On who is going to be the first to kiss you." She shook her head and smiled as she rolled her eyes. "The winner gets nearly a thousand dollars."

I laughed. That explained a lot, actually.

A week ago I was an unemployed teacher fresh out of college. Ready to take on the world, I could handle anything—at least, I'd thought I could. After less than a week here, I was beginning to regret my decision to teach high school students—especially when those students consisted only of hormonal teenage girls. This place was my idea of hell.

What the *fuck* had I been thinking?

Teaching at a prestigious girls' boarding school was a role I hadn't contemplated, nor did I think I'd ever stand a chance in hell of getting—and I probably wouldn't have, if it hadn't been for the headmistress being an old friend of my mother's. Yes, even though I was twenty-three, Mom was still interfering in my life. One call had gotten me an interview, and from there I had scored the job. My perfect grades, outstanding recommendations, and great outlook on life were just what they needed, apparently.

It was ironic, all things considered, that they saw me as a fresh, look-on-the-bright-side kind of guy when the reality was so different. I guess I was better at internalizing my feelings than I thought.

I looked at the girl again, trying to place her. She was in one of my classes, but so early on, all the girls blended into one another.

That's right. Wrenn . . . something.

Quiet and studious, she was one of the few girls I had crossed here who seemed to have some sort of plan for her future. Of course, that assessment was based off a couple of lessons and one homework assignment, but I got the feeling that most of the girls couldn't plan past their outfits for the next weekend.

"You're in my history class, right?" I asked her.

She nodded and smiled, adjusting the strap on her backpack over her shoulder. "Wrenn. I'm in your Monday morning and Thursday afternoon classes. History and Sociology." She blushed suddenly, her eyes growing wide with horror. "I'm not part of the pool," she added quickly.

I laughed as her face went red.

"I mean, not that I don't think you're attractive, but—"

"It's okay," I interrupted—mostly to stop her from digging a deeper hole for herself. "Just quit while you're ahead." I chuckled as she cringed again. "Anyway, I appreciate the heads up." I winked and walked past her down the now empty hall. "See you Monday," I called.

I made my way to the teacher's lounge, thinking about what Wrenn had told me.

A betting pool.

God, as if things weren't hard enough, now there was money on who could make me act inappropriately first? I'd had girls requesting one-on-one tutoring, girls leaving me gifts on my desk, and the number of girls "dropping" things while I was in their close proximity so they would have to retrieve them, asses high in the air, would almost be funny if it were happening to anyone else.

Hell, one girl had her father make a sizeable donation to the History department, stating that my techniques had encouraged his daughter to take her education more seriously. I'd been here a week! She was taking something seriously, but I doubted very much that it was her *education*.

Taking my lunch out of the fridge, I smiled and sat down next to Mark. At twenty-seven, he was four years older than me, yet the only one even remotely close to me in age. Every other teacher here was over thirty—with some having taught at the school for more than thirty years. Talk about feeling out of place.

Don't get me wrong. Everyone was nice, but the difference in age made it difficult to evolve relationships beyond the usual small talk. At least with Mark I could talk about football, or cars, and whatever else. The other teachers and their talk of politics and evolution intimidated the shit out of me.

My first impression of Tennerson Academy had been *holy fucking shit.*

Tennerson has consistently been in the top twenty preparatory schools in the country. As a senior school, it accepted students aged between sixteen and eighteen.

It had been exclusively a boarding school until 1983, when it began accepting day students as well. Today, the hundred and thirty-eight residential students were divided among five houses—each house accommodating up to twenty students. In each building there was a leader and two teachers. The remaining teachers either lived on or off campus.

As a new teacher, I was living on campus in my own unit, which somewhat resembled a hotel suite—modern and clean—located in the teachers' quarters.

Thank *fucking* Christ they hadn't put me in one of the residential houses. I wouldn't rule out being attacked in my sleep by some of these girls—girls who were used to getting exactly what they wanted.

This was so much more pressure than your usual teaching job. Here, you're around it 24/7. That's a hard thing to adapt to when you lack experience.

All you had to do was look around the teacher's lounge: Tennerson's liked experience, and *lots* of it. That made me feel nervous—like everyone was wondering what I did to get the job. Hell, I sometimes wondered *myself* how I got this job.

Oh wait, that's right: my interfering mother.

"Tuna fish?" Mark screwed his nose up as he glanced over at my sandwich.

"*You* don't have to eat it," I told him, taking a big bite and washing it down with a soda.

"Yeah, but I have to smell it," he retorted, moving a seat down.

I rolled my eyes at him. "Are you going to Layna's tonight?" I asked him. Layna—the headmistress—and her husband, Dan, lived in a house behind the main building. Every Friday night, she and Dan hosted a dinner for the staff.

I'd known Layna for years, though we had only met a handful of times at big family events. She and Mom spoke regularly, but living so far away from each other made catching up hard. It was those big events—like Dad's funeral—where I had actually met her.

Mark nodded. "Probably. Nothing better to do, may as well get a free feed, huh?"

"My thoughts exactly." I chuckled.

"Glad your first week is over?" he asked.

I groaned. "That would be an understatement. I just found out there's a betting pool on which one of my students is going to kiss me first."

Mark laughed, banging his fist down on the table. I glowered at him. Was it really *that* funny?

"Seriously? Watch out, dude, these girls are brutal. That's the trouble with rich kids—they're used to getting whatever they want, no matter the cost." He glanced down to his beer belly. "Not sure why they're not trying to hit me up, though." He grinned.

"No idea, dude." I laughed. "But I have to admit, I'm glad this is only a short-term contract."

"You say that now, but give it ten years. A pretty girl paying attention to you then will be the highlight of your week." He laughed again as I shook my head. There were so many things wrong with what he'd just said that I didn't even know where to start.

"I don't know about that, but I do wish girls had paid this much attention to me in college." I chuckled.

Mark snorted. "I find it hard to believe college girls were doing anything other than throwing themselves at your feet. And think about this: all those pretty college girls you were fucking last year? They were *these* girls only a year or two earlier."

I rolled my eyes as Mark guffawed loudly. He was trying to wind me up, but there was some truth to his comment, and it made my inexperience and close age to these girls even *more* obvious to me.

Last year I wouldn't have blinked an eye at the thought of making out with a hot freshman. Hell, my friends and I used to *prey* on 'fresh meat' as they called them.

They *would* be these girls in a few short months, and guys just like me would be all over them. I stood up, tossing my half-eaten sandwich in the garbage can, suddenly not that hungry.

I sighed, thankful there were only eight weeks of the school year left.

Surely I could handle eight little weeks?

Chapter Four

Dalton

The one good thing about living on campus? Two minutes and I was home.

Back in L.A., I'd still lived at home with Mom and spent half the day in the car getting to and from my classes. Here, I could get up fifteen minutes before my first class and still be early.

I made my way over to my unit on foot, crossing the sprawling green lawns that separated the school from the residential units. Trees lined the border of the entire property, most of them hundreds of years old, creating a feeling of privacy. My unit was in a cluster with fifteen others within an old, dated, red brick building.

Inside was a complete contrast. Everything had been remodeled, with modern new furniture, and finishes in grays and neutral tones. The living room was huge—as was the bedroom. The kitchen, though cramped, was complete with all the latest appliances. I even had a small balcony, which overlooked the entrance of the school.

I slapped my keys down on the counter and went straight for the fridge, grabbing a soda and some leftover pizza from the night before. Walking over to the sofa, I flopped down and flicked on the TV. My first week was officially over, and I had survived. Barely.

Eight more weeks.

If I could get through that, I could secure a job anywhere. That was what this was really all about: the security of a permanent job with benefits—such as health insurance—was something I needed. Not negotiable. This job on my resume was as good as a free pass to any teaching position I wanted. It put me one step above the other twenty thousand graduates who would be applying for the same positions I would be.

The dream to be a teacher had been with me for as long as I could remember and it was something that my father had *hated* when he was alive. I had so much potential, why did I want to waste it on a sub par career? Why didn't I want to follow in his footsteps and study Law? Why was I such a disappointment? Why wasn't I trying harder? All that when I was barely in middle school. Talk about pressure. In spite of all that, I knew he loved me and wanted the best for me.

When he found out he was sick, his entire outlook on life changed.

It had been a complete one-eighty turnaround. After his diagnosis, it was all about following my dreams, not settling for anything, and doing what made me happy.

Happy? Happiness was overrated. How could I ever let myself truly be happy knowing how easily everything I worked for could be ruined? Happiness was a trait that had eluded me for a long time. The best I could do was try and float with my head above water and hope I didn't drown, and some days even that was hard.

Some days, all I wanted to do was say 'fuck everything' and disappear, move some place where nobody knew me and start afresh. The only thing stopping me was Mom, and knowing I could never do that to her. Losing Dad had broken her. She couldn't handle losing me, too.

That, and I was smart enough to realize you can't run from your problems—they always catch up with you in the end.

***

Skype on my computer buzzed as I was getting ready to go out. It was Cam, one of my best friends from college and high school. Also a teaching graduate, he had ended up subbing for some of the roughest schools in Los Angeles. I reached over and clicked Accept, and turned on the mic.

"Hey man," I said, dropping into my seat.

Cam's big goofy grin filled the screen, his messy hair falling in all directions.

"How's it going?"

"Heeeeey. How's the private school boy going?" he yelled.

I sighed. "I can't wait for this to be over, actually. I'd rather be subbing in the worst school in the country than here. These girls are fucking insane, man," I said, stretching my arms behind my head.

Cam laughed. "Insanely hot, you mean. Am I right?" He laughed hysterically. Cam hadn't changed in the eight years I'd known him. He had way too much energy and nothing to burn it on. He was one of the most genuine people I knew, and had been such a support when my dad had died. At that stage we'd only been friends for a few months, but he was there for me when all my other friends deserted me, not knowing what to say or how to act. It was amazing how in the face of tragedy, it all became about them.

I shook my head. "Don't go there, man. God knows I won't be. How are you, anyway? Any more interviews?"

"Yeah, I had one yesterday for a pretty decent school not far from me, so fingers crossed, huh?" I heard a faint voice in the background. "Amy says hi."

"Hey Amy," I said back. Amy was his girlfriend of three years, and a real sweetheart. She kept him grounded. "Listen, I gotta go. A work thing, but I'll catch you soon, okay?"

"Sure, don't work too hard," he warned me.

"I never do," I shot back.

***

As I approached the house I adjusted my black sweater and my leather jacket, trying to steady my nerves. I wasn't a shy person by any means, but this was my first real job and I felt intimidated. I walked up the path leading to the porch and knocked on the door. Dan answered. He flashed me a grin.

"Dalton, good to see you again. Come in." He ushered me inside, patting me on the back. I followed him through to the patio out the back where the rest of the staff had gathered. "Can I get you a drink?" he asked, raising his eyebrows.

Dan was one of those guys I'd instantly liked when we'd first met. He was the type of guy who everyone liked. He was funny, social, friendly, and he worked hard—complete with stupidly long hours—in his job as head of the Engineering department at Hallbrook University, just a few towns over.

"Sure, just a soda will be fine, thanks."

This was one of those occasions where I wished I drank, just to calm my nerves. I stood awkwardly, smiling at anyone who made eye contact with me while I waited for Dan to return. I felt out of place, like the new kid in the playground. I'd literally spoken no more than a few words to these people. Some of them I didn't even recognize. Layna spotted me and waved me over.

At forty-two—the same age as Mom—Layna was tall, slim, and attractive. Her shoulder-length blonde hair was cut into a sharp bob that framed her angular face. Her piercing brown eyes made her look harsh—like someone you wouldn't want to cross. In reality, she was one of the most sincere, understanding people I'd ever met.

"Dalton." She smiled, touching my arm. "How are you settling in? Glad the week is over, I bet."

"Yeah, I'm loving it, but happy the weekend is here," I chuckled. Yes, a lie, but telling my boss how I really felt probably wasn't a great career move.

"Good to hear. Grab yourself a drink and mingle."

She took off, already talking to someone else before I could respond. Glancing around for Mark, I saw him standing by the bar, talking with the English teacher, Gary. I slipped out the door, trying to remember where the bathroom was from last week.

After I'd finished, I headed back toward the patio. Passing what looked like a living room, I heard the unmistakable sounds of Alfred Hitchcock's *The Birds* playing. I stopped and smiled.

God, I wish I was in there watching movies instead of trying to impress a bunch of strangers. I pushed the door open and ventured inside.

Wrenn sat sprawled out on a large leather recliner. Her eyes widened when she saw me. She sat upright, straightening her skirt. My eyes were drawn to her bare calves as she tucked them under her thighs.

"Mr. Reid," she said, her lips curving into a smile. She pointed to the TV. "Sorry, is it too loud?"

I jumped at the sound of her voice, forcing myself to focus on her face.

Great, now I feel like a creep.

But I was a twenty-three-year-old guy, and she was a pretty teenage girl who was only a few years younger than me. It was in my DNA to appreciate that.

"No, not at all," I replied, stepping further into the room. "And call me Dalton. We're not in class. Anyway, I was just passing, and I had to see who was watching one of my favorite movies."

"You're a Hitchcock fan?" She grinned, her face lighting up.

"More of a classic horror film buff," I said, sitting down on the edge of the leather armchair nearest to the door.

"Really? So am I. Nothing better than a horror movie that actually focuses on the story, you know? All the horror flicks these days seem to just be slash, blood, and gore." She shuddered and shook her head.

I laughed. She was right. Horror films today had nothing on their older counterparts; it just wasn't an argument I was used to hearing from someone under the age of fifty.

"So, I didn't realize you were going to be here," I said casually. There was really no polite way of asking her what the hell she was doing here.

She blushed. "Layna is my aunt. I live with her. That's why I'm at this school," she explained.

"Wow, I didn't know that," I said.

Wrenn looked at me strangely.

"My mom and Layna are old friends. They went to school together," I explained.

"Then your mom probably knew my mom," she said quietly. Her eyes dropped.

I'd obviously hit a nerve, and I noticed her use of past tense when talking about her mom. *What happened?*

"So, how do you like it here? A bit of a change from what you're used to?" she asked, a less than subtle change of subject.

I laughed. "Different is an understatement. I thought I knew what to expect. Honestly, the reality is *so* much worse," I said. "I'd forgotten how many hormones teenage girls have."

And there was something to add to my list of things not to say to my teenage student.

"Forgotten?" she teased. "Weren't you just in college, like, last year? Didn't they have teenage girls there?" She bit her lip to keep from smiling, her green eyes sparkling.

"You're right, but it wasn't my job to control them," I said, laughing.

"Yes, and they seem to go even crazier all cooped up in boarding school." She rolled her eyes. "This is my outlet," she added, gesturing to the TV. "Horror movies. It's a good escape. And often less scarier than reality," she quipped.

"If you like this you should try and get your hands on *Dawn of the Dead*. That's one of the best horror movies of all time," I said, ignoring how nerdy I sounded.

"Thanks for the tip," she said with a grin. "You better get back." She pointed to the door, her eyes piercing me. "They'll come looking for you."

"Yeah. I should," I muttered. *Even though I'd much rather stay in here.* "I guess I'll see you on Monday?"

"I guess you will. 'Night, Dalton."

Chapter Five

Wrenn

My pulse quickened as he walked into the room. God, he was driving me insane and he didn't even know it. Like right now, for instance: his ass in those jeans…

Sigh. That was probably the best thing about being a girl—I didn't have to worry about trying to hide an erection in the middle of class. I didn't know how boys did it. He set his briefcase down on his desk, flinging it open and taking out a stack of papers. Glancing around the room, he smiled.

"Good morning. Did we all have a good weekend?"

Murmurs filled the room. I was too busy staring at him to answer. His gaze swept past me, and for a moment I thought I saw a smile. Had that been for me? Was he thinking about running into me at Layna's?

Seeing Dalton out of class on Friday had been amazing. Sure, it had only been a five-minute conversation, but he'd treated me like a person. Every other teacher here knew my story, and all I ever got from them were sympathetic glances and those tiny little smiles that say "I'm not going to tell you how sorry I am for you, but I feel *so* sorry for you."

Ugh. It was like I couldn't escape my past, no matter how badly I wanted to. Thank God none of the other students knew—not even Kass.

The last thing they needed was more ammunition to use against me. The days they ignored me were best; I could handle that. It was the days they decided to pick on me relentlessly that were the worst. By 'they,' I meant Paige, but if she was targeting you, then everyone followed. It was sad, really.

It was amazing what a sexy, young, hot male teacher could do for your motivation levels. In the few months I'd been at this school, nobody had paid attention quite like they did in Mr. Reid's presence.

I studied the cause of this phenomenon as he waffled on about…honestly? I had *no* idea what he was talking about right then, and I was pretty sure every other student in the room felt the same way. He wasn't just attractive, he was down right freaking hot. Surely there was a law against a guy this gorgeous teaching teenage girls? This was a form of torture. But all the same, I'd take it. *Yep. I could get used to this.*

I sat back, my eyes on him as he took in the room. Again, I swear he smiled as his gaze swept past me. I couldn't have imagined that twice.

"How did everyone do with the homework I assigned?" he asked, sitting on the edge of his desk.

That's right, in my moment of appreciating the swooniness of my teacher, I'd forgotten we had an assignment due—just like the rest of the class had. The sound of papers rustling filled the silence as everyone dug through their folders. I pulled my three-page summary on the *Magna Carta* and passed it toward the front.

Out of the corner of my eye I saw Paige glance at me, then whisper something to her sidekick, Deena. They both giggled. I forced myself not to react. As much as I pretended I didn't care, it still hurt. Nobody wants to be the outcast.

You don't wake up in the morning and think to yourself, "Gee I hope they've vandalized my locker again today," or, "I hope they try and frame me for cheating on another test." I have no idea what I did to make Paige hate me so much, but whatever it was, in her mind it must have been big.

The rest of the period went quickly. I suppose time flies when you're not really listening. There were perks to repeating my senior year. Well, I wasn't really *repeating,* I guess. After the accident, it took me a long time to recover—both physically and mentally. Some things that were covered here I'd already covered in my old school, and some things I hadn't. It all depended on the syllabus. Either way, it would help me get the grades I needed to secure my place in prelaw at Boston University, and it meant I could graduate midyear.

The bell sounded, scaring the daylights out of me. My heart was still pounding as Mr. Reid dismissed us. As I packed up my things and began to walk out, he called me over.

"Wrenn, can I see you for a moment?" he asked casually. I nearly fainted.

Calm down, Wrenn. He probably wants to tell you off for not listening in class.

I smirked at Paige, who was giving me a death stare. I watched her flounce out of the room, knowing I'd probably be paying for that later.

Approaching the desk, I waited as he reached into his briefcase and pulled out a DVD. He handed it to me and I took it curiously, my fingers brushing past his as they wrapped around the hard plastic casing.

Holy shit.

I forced myself to focus on the DVD and not the electricity pulsating through my veins from his touch. *Did he feel that?* God forbid if he ever actually touched me—I'd probably orgasm on the spot. I studied the cover of the DVD.

Dawn of the Dead

"Ah, this is the one you were talking about?" I asked, suddenly excited. I flipped it over to read the back.

He nodded, his eyes studying my reaction.

I grinned, secretly happy that he had remembered me.

"If you can handle this one, then I have a few others that are pretty good too."

I raised my eyebrows at him. "You think I'm going to hide under the bed or something?" I teased him. "All I watch is horror movies, Mr. Reid. I'm *pretty* sure I can handle this little thing." I winked at him.

He laughed, running his hand through his hair, that beautiful smile appearing on his face. Ugh, he was making me weak at the knees.

Wrenn, say something else! I opened my mouth, and then closed it again. *Great, now I look like a freaking goldfish.*

"Okay, well, we'll see. I mean, this makes *The Birds* look like a comedy."

"Uh-huh," I said, still not convinced. I pushed the DVD into my backpack and smiled at him. "Well, thanks. Maybe I'll see you tomorrow at my aunt's?" I said, raising an eyebrow.

"Maybe," he murmured, holding my eye contact.

***

"So, what did he want?" pressed Kassia.

I laughed. I was barely out of the door when she pounced on me.

"Did you see Paige? Pissed off, is all I can say. You better watch your back."

"He just wanted to see how much of the syllabus I'd already covered in my old school," I fibbed. I didn't like lying to Kass, and I wasn't even sure why I did. All I knew was that I felt like I wanted to keep our little connection to myself—for a while, at least.

Kassia looked disappointed. "Is that all?" she said, glumly.

"What were you expecting? That he swept the junk off his desk and threw me down?" I snorted.

Kass grinned at me. "Well, I like that idea. Not only the idea of him doing that to you, but *me* doing that to you. Or maybe both him *and* me."

I shoved her playfully, knowing she was messing around. She had a girlfriend, Trina, who she'd been with for the last six months. Trina didn't go to Tennerson. She went to a public school in town, which was part of the reason Kass didn't live on campus this year.

Kass's parents were very cool. They accepted her sexuality, and loved Trina, and me, like we were part of the family. Which felt good. Especially those times when I missed my own family, so much. Layna was great, but she reminded me so much of my mother that when I was at my most down it was hard to be around her. If you'd seen them side by side, you'd pick right away that they were sisters. They had shared the same blonde hair and brown eyes. Both Jordan and I had taken after my dad, and Mom had hated that. She used to say she felt left out, because we all looked so alike.

"Come on. Let's get out of here. I'll have you back in time for dinner." She linked her arm through mine. I nodded my agreement and whipped out my phone to text Layna and let her know where I was going.

As we reached the parking lot, we were confronted by Paige, Deena, and Stacie, all three of them blocking our path. Paige stood in front, hands on her hips, her lip curled up in disgust

"Well if it isn't the two lesbian lovers," she sneered, as the other two girls giggled. Apparently anyone who spent time with Kass was a lesbian by association. Kass stepped forward until she was almost nose to nose with Paige.

"Get out of my way now, Paige."

"Or what? What are you going to do, Kass? Run off and cry into the arms of your little lover?" She thrust her finger toward me.

I shook my head, anger boiling inside of me. This girl was such a nasty piece of work. I tapped Kass on the shoulder. "Come on. She's not worth it. Let's just go," I muttered, glaring at Paige.

"Yeah, listen to your girlfriend and run away, dyke."

Kass began to laugh as Paige stared at her, shocked. "You know what I think, Paige? I think deep down, you want me. I think you lie in bed at night imagining my fingers inside of you, teasing you. I think you're aching to feel my tongue sliding between your legs, and you know you'll never have me." She smiled sweetly and grabbed my hand, walking around the three of them, giggling to herself.

"That was brilliant," I cried as soon as we were out of sight. "Fucking awesome, Kass. You told her!" Secretly, I wished I had that kind of confidence. I'd love to take Paige down a peg or two.

Chapter Six

Wrenn

As I glanced out the window of Kass's Jeep, I thought about my future. And my past. And how I couldn't wait to leave this place.

"What made you decide to stay at Tennerson's?" I asked her. "I mean, I hate it but I don't have a choice. I know your parents would let you move if they knew how much shit Paige and her skanks put you through."

Kassia glanced at me. The urge to ask her that had come out of nowhere, and surprised us both.

"They're not as bad as they used to be." She shrugged. "Besides, Tennerson's is the best prep school in the state. If I want to retain my acceptance at Harvard, then I have to stick it out. I don't give a shit about those girls. I couldn't care less what they think of me. They are going to get a harsh reality check next year when they go to the university where daddy bought them their place, and they realize they're not the top shit anymore."

Wow. I wish *I* were that confident in myself.

I hated that I let what others thought get to me. I never used to be like that. It was like the accident had killed all my self-esteem.

I couldn't wait to get to college. I felt as though, right then, I was in limbo—waiting for my life to begin. Everything I thought I knew about life and love was gone, yet I couldn't move forward just yet. Or maybe I didn't want to move forward?

Moving on meant accepting that the past was never going to change. I wouldn't be having any more late night chats with Mom about the boys I was crushing on. Or having her comfort me when my heart got broken. I wouldn't have another argument with Jordan, or see him graduate from high school. And Dad wouldn't be there to walk me down the aisle on my wedding day. None of my family would be there to see me marry the man of my dreams. Moving forward was terrifying, and at the same time exciting. I was so scared of forgetting, yet desperate for closure. No wonder I felt so damn confused.

"Don't let her get to you, Wrenn. You're so much better than her. Remember that." Kassia gave me a smile as she turned the car into the parking lot. Of course she thought this was all about Paige. She didn't know about my past.

"Am I that obvious?" I asked, making a face.

She laughed and nodded.

"I know, you're right. I'll work on it," I promised, wishing it were that easy.

***

We met Trina in Starbucks. I stood in line to get our orders while the other two found a booth—and each othe,r it seemed. They certainly weren't shy about displaying their affection in public. They'd caught the attention of every guy in the place—two pretty schoolgirls making out? Who'd have thought?

Smirking, I turned back around to face the counter. The guy standing ahead of me turned.

It was Mr. Reid. *Dalton.*

"Hey," I said, tapping him on the arm. "Fancy meeting you here."

"Wrenn." His face lit up. He rolled his eyes at the line in front of us. "There's nothing I hate more than waiting. It's almost enough to make me walk out, but unfortunately my caffeine addiction wont let me."

I giggled. "Yeah, the things we do for our addictions."

He raised his eyebrows at me and I blushed. I hadn't meant for that to sound so dirty. "So let me guess . . . you're a straight-up espresso kind of guy."

He looked offended. "You think I'm that boring? I'll have you know it's a mocha double-strength latte, all the way."

I love the way his eyes twinkle when he jokes with me.

"Hey, me too!" I smiled.

He chuckled at my enthusiasm. "So, you're here alone?" he asked.

I shook my head, and pointed to Kass and Trina, who were still making out in the booth. I cringed, but he just laughed.

"Good to see you relaxing."

"You don't think I relax? I relax *too* much. I'm the queen of procrastination," I proclaimed.

He smiled and raised his eyebrows. *Great, he doesn't believe me.*

"You seriously think I need to relax?"

"You always look so serious in class. I know, I've only been there a little over a week, but it's just the vibe I got from you. You work hard."

"At school, yes, I'm focused, because I know where I want to be and what I need to do to get there. Not only that, but school doesn't exactly fill me with feelings of happiness." I paused, realizing I was teetering on the edge of being too forthcoming. "I get bullied a lot, so I don't enjoy school. It's simply a means to an end for me. Nothing about that place fills me with warm fuzzy feelings."

"You handle it remarkably well," he offered. He paused, his expression becoming serious. "If it makes you feel any better, I used to get bullied, too."

"You?" I said, arching my eyebrow. I wanted to roll my eyes. This was as bad as those celebrity specials on TV where they all share their sob stories about being bullied as kids.

"Yes, me." He laughed. "What, you don't think a hip, cool guy like me could be teased?"

I blushed again.

Hip? I was thinking more along the lines of hot…sexy…amazing…

"You blush a lot, Wrenn. You should really get that under control. It gives away everything," he said with a wink. And just like that, he was next in line.

He placed his order, and then turned around. "What are you girls having?"

I relayed our order to the cashier. We stood off to the side together to wait for our drinks.

"You didn't have to buy our coffees," I said shyly. "I wouldn't want to get you into any trouble."

"It's coffee, Wrenn, not a joint," he smiled and I blushed again. God, I *did* need to work on my blushing. He chuckled, and shook his head as I ordered.

We stood next to one another, waiting. Could he see how nervous he made me? I was a wreck. My hands were shaking, my mouth was dry, and I couldn't stop thinking about how wonderful he smelled.

The barista placed our coffees on the counter. Dalton smiled at me as he reached for his.

"Have a good day, Wrenn."

Carrying our drinks over to the booth, Kass stared at me, her eyes narrowed.

"Was that our hot teacher I saw you talking to?" she accused.

"You came up for air long enough to see that, huh?" I grinned, setting down the tray. Trina laughed and reached for her cup.

"Yes. So was it?"

"Yes. He was in front of me, so we chatted." I shrugged innocently.

"Do you think he's hot?" she asked with a giggle.

I rolled my eyes.

"Oh, do you! You're hot for teacher! Go for it Wrenn, slut it up and make him want you."

"Shut up," I said, giving her the finger.

She laughed, taking a sip of her latte.

"I'm not going to throw myself at him like the rest of the school population." I was happy just admiring the view from a distance.

Chapter Seven

Dalton

"Mr. Reid, can I get help with this?"

I glanced up. Paige Warner stood in front of me, her hands resting on my desk.

"What's up, Ms. Warner?"

"This homework assignment—I wondered if you could have a look at it for me and make sure it's okay?" She leaned over, her blonde hair falling over her shoulder as she tilted her head, eyeing me seductively.

"Paige, this is due today. There's not much you can do at this point if it's not correct."

Her face went red.

I stood up and clapped my hands together. "Okay, guys, take your seats." My eyes swept over Wrenn in her usual spot in the back row. I gave her a wink, and she smiled.

Grabbing the handful of papers on my desk, most covered in red pen, I began to hand them out.

"Your homework assignments from last week. A few of you did really well. Some of you need to put a little more effort into your studies." I dropped a C-graded paper on Paige's desk. "Perhaps if you spent as much time on your homework as you did on shopping, this would be an A." Sniggers filled the room as she scowled at me. I placed Wrenn's paper down on her desk: A+.

"Good work," I said to her with another wink. She blushed, tilting her head as she gazed up at me.

"Yeah, it's not that hard to get good grades when your aunt pays the teachers' wages," muttered Paige. Her comment was greeted with laughter from the other students.

Wrenn stared down at her paper, refusing to bite.

"Enough, Paige," I snapped. "One more comment like that, and you'll fail my class. Are we clear?"

Her jaw dropped as she narrowed her eyes at me. She muttered a *yes*.

"Hand this week's assignment up to the front, and open your books to page seventy-three," I snapped, shooting another glance in Wrenn's direction. Her head was still down.

I glanced around the room. Some students eyed me with awe, impressed by my ability to shut Paige up. Others didn't look so impressed. Wrenn wore a tiny smile on her lips that made my heart skip.

Made my heart skip? What was I, a twelve-year-old girl?

Never mind the fact that any kind of heart-skipping behavior caused by a student was totally inappropriate. Wherever my heart—or any other parts of my body for that matter—was going with this, it needed to stop.

The bell rang and the girls began to pack up their things. While everyone else shot out of the room as quickly as possible, Wrenn seemed to be taking her time, handling each pen one by one as she placed them neatly in her backpack. By the time she stood up, the room was nearly empty, the last of the students filing out.

From the corner of my eye, I caught Paige glaring in my direction as she stomped out of the room. That girl made me shudder. One look at Paige and all I saw was trouble.

Wrenn, still smiling, approached the desk. Her green eyes were so bright with warmth that I couldn't help but feel good.

"Thanks for that. What you said to Paige." She paused, sweeping her hair over her shoulder. "But don't underestimate how much trouble that girl is. Even for you."

"I appreciate your concern, but I think I can handle it," I chuckled. If Paige wanted to learn how tough I could be, I was more than happy to show her. Girls like her made my skin crawl. She had no empathy or feelings for anyone but herself.

"Okay, if you say so." She smiled at me, her finger tracing the edge of my desk. I could feel my heart begin to race, and I had no idea why. I refused to believe it was because of her.

"You shouldn't be afraid to stand up to her, Wrenn."

She looked up, surprised, her eyes meeting mine. Then she shrugged, as if it were no big deal.

"Standing up for myself would just create more drama. I'd rather not have to deal with that. I've got bigger things on my mind than Paige and her petty comments." She smiled wistfully. "I'd rather focus my attention on the people I actually give a damn about. Does that make sense?"

"Perfect sense, actually," I mumbled, rubbing my neck, her comments hitting a little too close to home. "So, you're from Washington, and you like horror movies. What else is there to know about Wrenn?" I don't know why, but I didn't want her to leave yet. I wanted to keep this conversation going for as long as possible, without seeming like a complete creep.

She made a face, looking deep in thought.

"There's not much to know," she said truthfully. "I'm pretty boring, I guess. I love cars, and I hate shopping. I love things that make me think, like a good book. I'm quite opinionated, but I pride myself on seeing both sides of the argument. And I've wanted to be a lawyer since I was little."

"Any particular area of law?"

"Criminal law. Prosecution," she answered immediately. She glanced down at her phone. "And I'm late for class," she added sheepishly.

"I'll write you a hall-pass so you don't get into to trouble." I grinned, grabbing my pad. I scribbled out the note and handed it to her. Our fingers brushed against one another, her touch leaving me numb. She smiled at me, tiled her head down, and then walked out of the room.

Sinking back into my chair, I tried to process what had just happened. What was I doing? Creating little fantasies in my head over a student was just plain wrong. But there was something about her, something different. Something special that made me want—no, *need*—to know more.

Chapter Eight

Wrenn

I found myself looking forward to History classes much more than I should have. After two weeks of Dalton being in my life, any chance I got to see him was something I looked forward to.

A schoolgirl crush? Maybe. I wasn't sure.

In class he always treated me the same as everyone else, but unlike some of my other teachers, he didn't sit back and ignore Paige's snarky comments. There was no special treatment toward me—perhaps I imagined a glance here and a smile there, but nothing concrete. Out of class, he treated me like an equal.

It was something that would never go anywhere, but it gave me comfort to think about him as being something more than just my teacher. I didn't for a second dream that my crush would be reciprocated. I wasn't stupid. He had been nothing but above board when he was with me, in and out of class.

Still, I couldn't stop myself from fantasizing about him when I lay in bed at night, or imagining what it would be like to kiss him. As each day progressed, I found myself thinking about him more and more.

***

I practically skipped to class on Thursday, which earned me an odd look from Kass. She never saw me this happy about school, so I didn't blame her skepticism.

"What the hell is with you?" she asked, raising her eyebrows.

Shit. I needed to settle down. Nobody was this excited about History. "Nothing. Just feeling good today. Being almost the weekend, and all."

She seemed to accept that and proceeded to ramble on about her plans for the weekend.

"Wrenn?"

"Huh?" I said, embarrassed that she had caught me lost in thought.

"I said you should come with us. Up the coast."

This weekend? Hanging around the school gave me the chance to possibly see Dalton. I wasn't about to give that up. *Besides, a weekend away with those two, watching them make out?*

I think I'll pass.

"I promised I'd help my aunt with something," I fibbed, biting my lip. The chances of running into him were small, but I'd still take it. Besides, I knew Kass and Trina enjoyed their alone time.

Kass nodded. "Too bad. If you get out of it, let me know. It'll be fun."

We walked into the room, taking our usual seats in the back. Dalton was there already. Paige and her sidekick, Deena, stood next to him, giggling and flicking their hair. I almost chuckled at how uncomfortable he looked. Obviously his handling of her behavior on Monday hadn't dampened her interest in him. His eyes caught mine and narrowed slightly as I giggled. It was those little connections we had, like just then, that made me wonder…

"What's funny?" Kass asked, interrupting my thoughts.

"Paige and Deena. Look at how awkward Mr. Reid looks."

Kass glanced over at them and began to snigger loudly. Paige glared back at us, her expression one of pure hatred.

"Okay guys, settle down." Mr. Reid waited as the last few students scuffled into class and sat down. He held up some papers. "I have your assignments to give back. Some are excellent, and some of you need to focus more." He began to work his way around the room, handing back papers. He winked as he reached me, dropping my A+ paper down on my desk.

"Good job, again," he muttered softly. I couldn't help it, I was grinning like an idiot. Paige rolled her eyes, but didn't say anything. I didn't even care.

Even she couldn't ruin how good I felt right now.

***

"You wanna come to mine?" Kass bit down on her apple as we walked outside. It was overcast and cold, a typical day for this time of year. All I wanted to do was curl up in front of the fire with a book, or maybe a movie.

"Nah, I might have an early night. I'm exhausted." I yawned and stretched out my arms.

Kass rolled her eyes. "You're weak," she said with a grin as she walked toward the parking lot. "But okay. See you tomorrow!"

I spent the evening stretched out on the sofa watching *Dawn of the Dead.* He was right: it was a damn good movie, and scary as hell. My stomach somersaulted when I thought about him. He'd gone out of his way to lend me this movie. Did he mean anything by it? Or was he just being nice? I was trying so hard not to read into every little interaction because I just knew I was setting myself up to be hurt. I was his student. He was my teacher. *That* was the only thing I knew for sure.

Chapter Nine

Wrenn

Wow, I was exciting.

Saturday night and I was at home, studying. My aunt and uncle saw more action than I did. They had gone out for the afternoon—and evening—to a wedding.

Kass had asked me again to go with her and Trina, but I honestly just felt like staying home. I liked having the house to myself, and studying meant my mind was kept occupied. When my mind was occupied, I didn't dwell on the past. It was that simple.

Hearing the doorbell, I ran downstairs to answer it. I swung the door open and gaped in surprise. Dalton stood there, looking devilishly sexy in a pair of jeans and a Jacket. He flashed me that gorgeous crooked smile. He looked pleased to see me.

"Wrenn, hey. Is Layna home?" He held up a small package wrapped neatly with a bright pink ribbon. "A present from my mom," he explained with a sheepish grin. I giggled. That was *so* cute.

I stood aside and let him in. Shutting the door, I motioned for him to go through to the kitchen.

"She and Dan are at a wedding. Can I get you a drink?" I asked.

He hesitated, and then nodded. "A soda would be nice, thanks." He placed the present down on the counter, watching me as I poured two glasses of soda. *Could he see how much my hands were shaking?*

I handed him one of the glasses and smiled, taking a sip as I walked over to the table. He followed, sliding into the chair opposite me.

Is this really happening?

Dalton, alone with me in my house, inches away from me. I could stretch my leg out right now and it would accidentally brush past his. Not that I would. My heart was racing, and I was shaking like crazy. Could he see how nervous he made me? Fuck, I hoped not. I wanted to exude calm and cool, not a hot mess.

"I thought the entire student population would be out tonight, being a Saturday night," he said lightly, his eyes on mine.

I shrugged and fiddled with the rim of my glass, the tip of my finger going round and round. I glanced up and caught him staring. He looked flustered when his eyes met mine.

"What can I say? I'm boring," I said with a smile. "I was accepted into prelaw at Boston University, but it's a provisional acceptance dependent on my grades. Any spare time I have goes into that."

"And scary movies," he added, his eyes twinkling.

I laughed. "Yes. Speaking of which…" I stood up, my drink in hand, waving for him to follow me.

He raised an eyebrow and looked at me suspiciously.

"I'm taking you into the living room. I'm not planning on assaulting you," I joked.

His face flushed, which only made me giggle harder.

Worst attempt at humor ever. Someone needs to stop me. Intervention please.

In the living room, I set down my drink and reached for the stack of DVDs on the coffee table.

"This is yours," I said, handing him back *Dawn of the Dead*.

"Did you enjoy it?" he asked.

"Loved it," I admitted. I handed him the rest of the DVDs. "And these all came yesterday, express mail." I'd gone more than a little crazy ordering up on Amazon.

"Holy shit, nice choice," he said, holding up my copy of *Rosemary's Baby*.

"I've never seen it," I said with a smile.

He gasped, shaking his head in mock horror. "And you call yourself a horror buff? Fuck homework. You need to watch this now. Right now," he declared. "Even if it means you don't get into college, it'll be worth it. It's imperative you see this movie."

"Why don't you stay? Layna and Dan will be a while, still, and if it's as scary as you say it is, there is no way in hell I'm watching it alone." *Ha, bullshit.* I lived for horror movies, but I wasn't letting him leave without a fight.

He hesitated for half a second, and then shrugged. "Okay, what the hell. Let's do this."

I tried to contain my excitement. He said yes? I had so *not* expected him to say yes! My excitement turned to horror as it sank in. *Holy shit, how can I sit next to him for two freaking hours and sixteen minutes?*

"If you put it on, I'll order a pizza," he said, decisively. "Any particular kind?" he asked.

I shook my head.

He fished out his phone and called the delivery place while I fiddled with the DVD player, my stomach feeling like it was home to a rave full of moths on acid.

Why moths? Because they aren't as graceful as butterflies.

I sat down in one of the leather recliners, tucking my feet up under me. I studied him while he was on the phone and unaware of my attention. His dark hair was messy, but it worked perfectly with his jeans and faded shirt. He wore a black jacket, which looked like leather. I resisted the urge to reach out and touch it.

Everything about him I wanted to touch: his hair, I wanted to run my hands through; the stubble on his jaw, I wanted to feel on my fingertips, his lips, I wanted to feel pressed against mine, his tongue invading my mouth. Oh God, he was making me wet . . .

"Ten minutes," he said, jolting me out of my daydream. *Ten minutes, what? Oh, the pizza...*

"Okay. Well, we can start the movie now, anyway."

He settled down in the armchair next to me. *God, I can smell his aftershave.* That citrus, woody tone mixed with the sweet scent of his sweat. Was it wrong that I just wanted to lean over and sniff him? I giggled, the mental image too funny to resist. He glanced at me, brow creased, and shook his head.

He probably thinks I'm a freak.

I had this strange habit of spontaneously laughing when I was nervous, and nothing made me more nervous than having him as close to me as he was right then. I was sure I was coming across as an immature teenager.

What was I doing, asking him to stay and watch a movie with me? And why had he agreed? Isn't Rule One of teaching *not* to associate with your students outside of class? The fact that he was in my living room, his hand inches from mine, made me nervous. Moments ago this had all been a silly crush in my head, but the possibility of this actually going somewhere scared the hell out of me.

In my fantasies, I'd imagined myself taking the lead and seducing him. He'd be unable to resist my charms.

In reality? Fuck, no. There was *no* way I could ever make a move.

No fucking way. I felt nervous changing positions in my seat, for God's sake. I'd never have the guts to try something . . . would I?

The doorbell rang and I jumped. Dalton chuckled as I pressed Pause.

"You can't even handle the doorbell. How the hell are you

going to handle the scary parts?" he teased, standing up.

I glowered at him as he left the room. A few minutes later he came back in, pizza box in hand, with two cans of soda. I pushed aside the books scattered on the coffee table as he set down the box.

"Here," he said, tossing me one of the cans.

I caught it. "Thanks," I said, sitting it on the table next to my half-full glass of Coke.

He opened the lid and presented the box to me. I picked the slice with the most pepperoni.

"I was going to go that one," he said, narrowing his eyes at me playfully.

"Too bad. You shouldn't have offered it to me first, then." I shrugged, shoving it in my mouth.

"Really? I guess that's what I get for trying to be a gentleman," he said, his lips breaking into a grin.

I rolled my eyes at him and took another big bite, trying to ignore that beautiful dimple on his cheek that I just wanted to reach out and touch. "Get over it," I joked, covering my mouth with my hand.

He laughed and reached for a slice. I unpaused the movie and he got right back into it, as though there'd been no interruption.

I paid more attention to him than I did the screen. I figured I could watch the movie again later. Watching *him* later would be a little more difficult—and creepy.

His eyes were glued to the screen as he shoved pizza into his mouth. I focused again on the fuzzy regrowth around his jaw line. Did he do that purposely, or could he just not be bothered to shave? I think that would be the thing that would annoy me most about being a man—having to shave every freaking day. It was an effort for me to wax once a month.

Downstairs, I had a basic bikini line wax and kept myself nicely trimmed. For the love of God, I couldn't understand why girls went completely bare. There was no way in hell I'd ever be doing that. I was a wuss when it came to pain.

I cringed. Was I seriously sitting here next to my teacher, thinking about Brazilians and pubic hair? *What the hell is wrong with me?* God, now I was thinking about what he'd like. I bet all the chicks he had been with were smooth and bare down there . . .

Snap out of it, Wrenn!

I blushed furiously, praying to God he wouldn't look over at me. He didn't.

***

"Well, I have to admit that was pretty damn good."

Dalton grinned as he stretched his legs out. "I can't believe you hadn't seen that before," he said, shaking his head.

"I imagine there are quite a few classics I've yet to see that I should have," I replied, running my hand through my hair. I sat forward and closed the empty pizza box. "Thanks for staying. This was fun."

"It was," he agreed, his gaze lingering on me, a tiny smile threatening to invade his mouth. "There aren't too many people here that I've been able to be myself around," he admitted. He sat forward, his arms resting casually on his legs. "I knew moving away from my friends and family would be hard, but it's harder than I thought."

"I can imagine," I said softly. My mind flashed back to all my old friends. I hadn't even heard from them, not since the accident.

"Of course," he said. "What am I saying? You know exactly how I feel. I suppose you rack up a huge phone bill, too, right? Thank God for Skype is all I can say."

"I don't exactly have many people to call," I replied carefully. Wow this was going downhill fast.

His face fell, and I knew he'd realized he had put his foot in it. I hadn't planned on explaining my situation to him so quickly, but now I felt like I had to.

"I moved here because . . . because my family was killed in an accident last year. Layna is my only living relative. She had to take me." I swallowed hard, praying he wouldn't press me for more details.

"Shit, Wrenn. I'm an idiot. I can't believe I said that." He buried his head in his hands.

"You didn't know," I said. "Most of the staff know, but only because they were here when I came here, and Layna thought it was best they knew, considering my fragile state. The students don't know. And I'm glad. They hate me enough as it is."

"Maybe them knowing would give them a better insight to who you are and what you've been though? I'm sure they don't hate you," he replied, his voice soft.

I laughed. "Trust me, they do. I'm the niece of the headmistress and I don't come from a family of big money. Add to that all the 'special' attention I used to get from teachers who were just trying to look out for me, and what's to not like?" I joked. I shrugged. "Not that I care. With the exception of Kass, I'd prefer not to know any of my peers. I focus on my schoolwork and grades. That's it. Two more months and I'm free. Less than two months. Six weeks. Thank God for extra credit and early graduation."

He was silent for a moment. "Anyone who chooses not to get to know you is missing out. Not you. You're unlike anyone I've met." He looked up and met my gaze; those incredible blue eyes were staring right into my soul. It gave me goose bumps. This guy made me feel like I wanted to live. Really live, not just go through the motions of day to day life.

I smiled, not sure how to respond to his comment. "You're just trying to be nice, and I appreciate that, but I know how little this place matters out there in the real world. What people here think of me, I try not to let it get me down. I just think of the future. A few more months and I'll be in college. Hell, if it weren't for the accident, I'd have been in college this year."

"You would?" he murmured, his brow furrowing at the thought.

"Yes. I'm repeating my senior year because of the accident. That's how I have enough credits to graduate midyear."

"Wow, I didn't realize," he mumbled, looking up at me and shaking off whatever train of thought had been distracting him. "Anyway, I'd better go. I can only imagine the gossip that would circulate if I was seen here when Layna wasn't home." He rolled his eyes and stood up, his phone shooting out of his hands and landing on the floor. We both bent down to retrieve it, almost banging heads in the process. For a second, we looked at each other. I couldn't read his expression.

He straightened up abruptly, giving me a tight smile. "I'll see you next week."

Chapter Ten

Dalton

If not for her accident, she would be a college student this year.

College. Not high school, but *college*.

Why did hearing her say that make me want to squirm? The same reason my heart dropped when she thought I was just being nice for telling her she was special. This girl was beginning to have an effect on me.

If Wrenn had been a freshman in college when I was there, would I have . . . ?

It doesn't matter. God, why am I even thinking that? She's not in college, and I'm not back there, either. Besides, even if things were different, god knows I don't do relationships.

I shouldn't have stayed. My intentions at first were completely innocent, and she'd given me no indication that she wanted anyone but someone to kill time with.

But the more I sat there, trying to watch that damn movie, the more my thoughts drifted to something more...inappropriate. Every shift she made on that damn seat next to me, every toss of her hair—sending another wave of her perfume my way—sent my mind into a spin. So many times I thought—fuck, I'd even *hoped*—that she was going to make a move. And as much as I wanted to invite her over to join me on the sofa, I kept thinking of how wrong it would be and I just couldn't do it.

For the entire two hours and sixteen minutes of *Rosemary's Baby*, I had an internal battle, back and forth, of asking her to join me on the sofa, and then ripping myself apart in the debate of how I'd tell her we couldn't cross that line. My head was one big mess.

Being alone in her house while she was my student was a big fuck-up on my part, and I couldn't let that happen again. What if someone had seen me? I'd be out of a job so fast I wouldn't know what hit me, and I could kiss my entire career goodbye.

Besides, what the hell did I think was going to happen? How easy it had been to forget the real reason my friends had called me "Solitaire" in college: because I never spent more than one night with the same girl. I couldn't do relationships. I'd never had one, and I probably wouldn't—not anytime soon.

But she was different. And she had been through so much. I

couldn't deny there was a connection, not to myself. The sorrow I'd felt for her when she told me about losing her family—I'd so badly wanted to take all the pain away. That urge to protect her was going to get me into trouble. I had to be careful.

If I was being honest with myself, my career was the least of my worries when it came to Wrenn.

***

The week passed by uneventfully. I focused on my work and tried to minimize the number of creepy stares I sent Wrenn's way during classes. Thank God most of them were when she had her head down, focusing on her work, or she'd have me up on a restraining order.

Paige and her snotty attitude toward Wrenn was beginning to irritate the hell out of me. Several times I had to bite back comments that would have been personal and downright nasty—*not* the way a teacher wants to react toward a student, but the way a man might protect his woman.

Wrenn, of course, handled Paige's nastiness the same way she always did: by ignoring it and focusing on the things that were important to her. God, I admired her strength so much.

Memories of my own childhood were brought back, flashing through my head. Being picked on because of Dad's disease had been frightening for a young kid. But even worse was the shame I felt for myself for asking him to drop me off around the corner from school, or to not attend my school events, all for fear of being picked on.

I will never erase the image of him on the day I told him I didn't want him to come to my middle school graduation. The pain in his eyes would be something that would haunt me forever. All because a couple of assholes made fun of me because of his disability.

I'd broken his heart that day and I'd never forget how that felt.

**

The days seemed to be flying past, and by Friday afternoon I was at home, getting ready to head back over to the teacher's lounge for a syllabus meeting. I decided to call Mom. I hadn't spoken to her more than a week, and I knew she liked hearing from me regularly. Picking up the phone, I dialed her number.

"Dalton," she said, sounding happy.

"Hey, Mom. How are you?" I asked, balancing the phone in the nook of my shoulder as I buttoned up my shirt.

"I'm good, honey. Just leaving work now. How's the job going? Are you enjoying it? I hope everyone is being nice to you."

"Work's fine, Mom, and yes, everyone is great," I chuckled. All she needed to know was I was fine and happy. She didn't need the full, drawn-out story.

"Good. I told Layna to keep an eye on you, you know."

"I'm aware of that, Mom," I replied, amused.

"I worry about you. That will never stop, you *know* that. Especially when we don't know—"

"Mom, I'm fine. Stop worrying about me," I said, cutting her off. "I have to go, but I'll call you soon, okay? I love you."

"Love you too, honey."

I hung up.

Sighing, I picked up the photo of Mom and Dad I had sitting on the desk. It was taken before he'd started showing symptoms. At two, I was supposed to have been in the photo, but wouldn't sit still. Every image came out the same: me running away, Mom with her hands on her head, and Dad screaming after me. This was one of my favorite pictures because it reminded me how important family was.

Chapter Eleven

Wrenn

I was beginning to notice things that I knew were not just in my head: the way he kept eye contact with me for half a second longer than he did everyone else, the fact that he would find any excuse to come over to the house. We could sit and talk for hours about nothing, and everything. He was still professional, he was still my teacher, but out of class he had become my friend.

Tonight, I was going to test this. He either felt something or he didn't, and if he didn't, then I'd be spending the rest of the semester embarrassed as hell every time I had to walk into that classroom.

"Anyone home?" I called out, dropping my books on the hall table.

Silence greeted me. My heart thumping, I made my way into Layna's office. I walked over to her desk and sat down, with no idea where to start. The slightest noise made me jump, because I was so sure I was going to get caught. I'd make the *worst* burglar.

I flicked though some papers and found nothing. The filing cabinet; nothing. The desk drawers; nothing. I was losing hope of ever finding what I needed when I saw it.

Her phone. She was forever leaving it at home. This was perfect. Her phone was the best chance of finding what I was looking for.

Picking it up, I clicked my way to Contacts and scrolled down to *Reid*.

And there it was. My hands shook as I copied the number into my phone. A voice in the back of my mind was screaming at me. *What the hell are you doing?* I clicked out of Contacts and navigated my way back to the main screen, setting the phone down exactly where I'd found it, right down to the angle it had been at.

Even once upstairs in the safety of my room, my heart was still racing. I sat down cross-legged on my bed, staring at the number. *His* number. Was I really going to do this? What if he brushed me off? I took a breath and dialed before I could change my mind.

"Hello?"

Oh my God. His voice sent chills through my body. I nearly ended the call. My voice wouldn't work, and I was beginning to sweat.

"Hello?" he repeated.

"Uh, hi," I managed. *Fuck, I'm an idiot.*

"Who is this?" he asked, his voice curious.

I slapped my hand over my face. *Oh God, kill me now.* This was getting worse by the minute.

"It's Wrenn."

"Oh." He sounded surprised. And guarded. "Can you hold for a moment?"

"Uh, sure," I mumbled. This was going really bad. I heard the muffled sound of him talking to someone. A few seconds passed, and then the sound of a door shutting.

"Sorry. I was . . . in a meeting. Are you okay?" he sounded concerned.

I felt so embarrassed. In what stupid fantasy had this seemed like a good idea? He was my teacher, he was five years older than me, and more than that, he was hot, sexy, and capable of getting *any* girl he wanted. Why would he be interested in *me*?

"Wrenn?"

"Um, I'm sorry. This was stupid . . . "

"What is it?" he pressed. Great. Now he sounded amused, like he thought this was funny.

Kill me now. I sighed. I already looked like a fool. How much worse could this get?

"*Psycho* is playing over in Hallbrook tonight, and I wondered if you wanted to go," I practically shouted the words down the phone. I slapped my hand over my mouth, so completely embarrassed.

"With you?" he asked, astonished.

"No, with the gardener," I retorted.

He chuckled, probably at the thought of grumpy old Mr. Landen enjoying anything in life, let alone a movie.

"Look, I just thought it might be something you'd like to do, you know, as friends, but it's probably a really bad—"

"Okay," he said, cutting me off.

Huh? Did I just hear correctly?

"Okay?" I repeated, stunned. Surely I must've heard him wrong.

"Yes. It's probably best you meet me there, though," he added awkwardly.

"Yeah, sure. So it starts at seven. I will meet you there ten minutes before?"

"Sounds good. I'll see you then."

Yep. I was grinning like an idiot.

Hanging up the phone, I fell back on the bed.

Holy shit.

A wave of nausea ran over me. What the hell was I going to wear? I jumped up and ran down to the bathroom, turning on the taps as I stripped out of my uniform. After soaping myself up, I stood under the stream of water, trying to calm my nerves.

He just sees me as a friend. He probably feels sorry for the poor little orphan with no friends. No matter how often I kept repeating it to myself, a small part of me wanted to scream at the top of my lungs. There was no stopping that part of Wrenn from getting her hopes up. That part of me kept piping up with ridiculous thoughts. Things like, *why would he risk his job to meet you for a movie if he just wanted friendship?*

Stepping out of the shower, I dried my hair and tied it back into a loose bun, my bangs falling forward and covering my forehead. I wrapped a towel around me and walked back to my room. Now I had to decide what to wear.

I shuffled through my underwear drawer for my nicest bra and thong; a cream-colored French lace set Kass had given me for my birthday, all the way from a trendy Paris boutique.

I was anything but a slut. I had no intention of letting anyone see my underwear today, or anytime soon, for that matter, but I felt good wearing it. Over the top of the bra I slid a dusky pink silk tank, which I paired with my skinny jeans, calf-high black boots, and my warm short black woolen jacket. Finally, I picked out a smoky gray eye shadow that made my eyes look bigger, and a soft pink lip-gloss.

Perfect: I looked sexy, yet casual enough for a movie with a friend. I grabbed my purse and raced downstairs to the kitchen.

On top of the counter, I scribbled a note:

Going out with Kassia, will be home by curfew.

Wrenn xx

I had a pretty decent curfew, considering I rarely had anywhere to go—midnight on weekends, and eleven on school nights, with staying over at Kass's fine anytime, as long as Layna knew where I was.

That was the only time when being the headmistress's niece came in handy. While any of the girls could leave for the night if they had parental permission, it was much easier for me to obtain if I just needed some space.

I climbed into my car and plugged the theater into my GPS. Hallbrook was two towns over, about a thirty-minute drive. The location was far away enough that we were unlikely to be spotted, especially since tonight was dinner night at the house for staff. Another reason I was surprised he had said *yes*. What would he tell my aunt?

It sure as hell wouldn't be the truth.

***

I pulled up outside the theater with five minutes to spare. Reaching into my purse, I clasped my hand over my compact, bringing it up to my face to check my makeup. I didn't wear it often, so it felt weird wearing it now, like there was something on my eyes that I needed to scratch off.

Taking a deep breath, I walked over to the entrance, looking around for Dalton. I spotted him standing to the left of the ticket box. His eyes lit up when he spotted me.

God, he looks so hot.

He wore faded blue jeans and a black leather jacket over a

gray T-shirt. His tousled light brown hair looked perfect, and his eyes were so blue I felt like I'd fall into them if I stared for too long.

"Hey, Wrenn." He smiled, his eyes so focused on mine, like he didn't trust himself to let them wander over my body. The thought sent shivers down my spine.

"Hey," I said warmly. "We should probably get our tickets." I glanced around the deserted entrance and frowned. "Though I would have expected more of a crowd." I walked up to a rather uninterested looking dude sitting in the booth.

"Hi. Two tickets for *Psycho*," I said.

"Wrong day, honey. That's tomorrow night." *Shit.* I turned around to see Dalton chuckling behind me. My desire to punch the ticket guy for calling me "honey" was washed away by my embarrassment about getting the day wrong.

"It's not funny," I grumbled, my cheeks glowing red. "I feel like an idiot." I was such a tool. Who gets the freaking day wrong?

"Come on, it is pretty funny." He tugged at my arm, making me look up at him. His smile was contagious, and pretty soon we were both laughing.

"Have you eaten?" he asked.

I shook my head.

Food? No, I'd been way too nervous for food.

"Okay. Let's get some dinner. There's a place just up off the highway that does a pretty decent meal. We can go in my car."

I nodded, following him, not quite able to comprehend that I was about to get in his car—alone.

Just him and me.

"Nice," I murmured, running my finger along the bonnet of the red Mazda rx7.

He razed his eyebrows, amused.

"What?" I said teasingly, "I'm not allowed to like cars?"

"No, it's not that at all." He shook his head. "It's just not many girls your age would even know what this is."

"My age?" I scoffed. "You're only a few years older than me."

"Six," he corrected, his eyes twinkling. "I'm twenty-three."

"Actually, smartass, five," I shot back.

"You're eighteen?" he said, his jaw dropping.

"Yes." I smirked. "Remember? I'm repeating this year. That makes me eighteen, and legal in many countries for various activities."

We both fell silent as we climbed into the car. *Did I really just say that?*

God, I needed a gag; anything to stop me talking. I buckled up my seatbelt, loving the feel of the low seats.

"You sure you can handle this thing?" I joked, trying to lighten the mood. It worked.

He winked at me as he revved the engine before slamming it into gear. I laughed as we took off down the street, smoke ripping up under the wheels. "Sorry. I guess I should be acting a little more responsibly, huh?" he chuckled, his eyes bright with excitement.

"I don't know, I'm liking this side of you. And besides, it's the weekend. You have to let your hair down sometime." I liked the idea of him letting his guard down around me. It told me that he didn't see me as a student. The thought made my stomach somersault.

***

"So, tell me about you. You love fast cars and horror movies; what else is there to know about Mr. Reid?" I asked, licking the last of possibly the best chocolate mousse I'd *ever* experienced off my spoon.

"Well, for one, my name is Dalton," he replied, narrowing his eyes at me.

"Okay, Dalton." I giggled. *Dalton*. I loved that name.

"It's just my mom and I. Dad died when I was fifteen. I've always wanted to be a teacher, though originally I wanted to go with elementary."

"Why did you go with high school?" I asked curiously.

He shrugged. "Last minute decision," he said with a smile.

I laughed. "Oh, I bet you're regretting that now," I teased.

"I have no idea what you mean." He looked at me innocently, and then his face broke into a smile. "Okay, teaching teenage girls is pure hell."

I giggled. "Come on, it can't be that bad. A couple of hundred girls, all thinking you're a god? That's got to boost the ego."

"A couple of hundred girls all under the age of eighteen," he corrected dryly.

"I'm not," I said lightly, surprised by what was coming out of my mouth.

"Yeah, well you're the exception," he said.

The exception. I liked being the exception. I met his gaze, his eyes burning into mine. My face began to heat. How could I not read into things when he was staring at me like that? I felt naked under his gaze.

Had I imagined the change in his behavior since he found out I was eighteen? Did that make a difference as to how off-limits I was?

"You know, given the right circumstances, we could have almost crossed paths in college," I began, my tone light. "I mean, if I was in college this year, and you had continued with your studies, like a PhD or something."

He nodded, those deep blue eyes boring into mine. "Do you have a point?" he asked, raising his eyebrows.

I shrugged. "I don't know. Would you have batted an eyelid at going out with a freshman? Probably not. I guess I'm just saying under different circumstances . . . " I let my voice trail off, hoping it sounded deliberate. In truth, words had deserted me.

Had I just propositioned my teacher? Yes, yes I had.

To my relief, he laughed. "You said you're going to study law, right?"

I nodded.

"That's good. You certainly give compelling arguments." He waved down the waitress and smiled at me. "I think we should get you back home before you get me in trouble."

***

He dropped me back at my car just before ten thirty. I was shocked at how late it was. We had been talking for hours. I felt so relaxed around him, yet at the same time nobody had ever had me feeling so damn wound up.

"So, you still want to see this movie tomorrow?" he asked, raising an eyebrow.

"Are you asking me out?" I asked, my tone sweet.

"No. I'm merely trying to broaden the cinematic knowledge of one of my students." His expression became serious. "Asking out one of my students would be incredibly unprofessional on my part, and unethical. I wouldn't take advantage of you like that."

"What if I wanted to be taken advantage of?" I moved toward him, very slowly, gauging his reaction. He held his breath as I edged closer, until our lips were almost touching. I paused, looking into his eyes, so desperately wanting to feel his lips against mine but not wanting to step over that boundary without him wanting it equally.

He tilted his head so his lips brushed over mine, the sensation making me dizzy. His hand wandered up to my face, his fingers gently running along my hairline. Then suddenly my lips were crushed up against his with a passion even *I* wasn't expecting.

As quickly as it began, he was away from me, his eyes a mixture of lust, regret, and confusion. I was a hot mess. My heart was beating out of control, I felt hot *and* cold and lightheaded. Thank God I was sitting down, or I was sure I'd have ended up fainting.

"I'm sorry, Wrenn. I shouldn't have done that," he said quietly.

"You didn't do anything I didn't want," I replied.

He sat, his hands clenched tightly on the steering wheel, not speaking.

"Will I see you tomorrow?" I asked.

He glanced at me, confused.

"The movie," I reminded him.

He exhaled loudly. "Do you think that's a good idea?" he asked, raising his eyebrows.

"Maybe not, but I think we need to talk about this . . . " My voice trailed off as he nodded.

"I'll call you." His voice had softened, as had his expression. His eyes were no longer hard.

I nodded and got out of the car, closing the door. He drove off, and I stood there on the curb, staring until I could no longer see his taillights. Once he was gone, I stepped into my car.

I sat there, trying to digest what had just happened. Kissing him had evoked everything in me. It felt like a hurricane of feelings and emotions had ripped through my body, leaving me a muddled mess inside.

I reached into my purse and pulled out my phone. It had been on silent since I'd arrived at the theater. There were six missed calls from Kassia, and countless texts, all conveying the same message; *call me.*

I dialed her number. She answered on the first ring.

"Where the hell have you been?" she shrieked loudly.

"What's wrong?" I asked, alarmed at her tone.

"What's wrong? Fuck, Wrenn. If you're going to tell your aunt you're going out with me, at least clue me in on it." She sounded frustrated and annoyed.

Shit.

I hadn't even considered the fact that Layna was friends with

Kass's parents.

"Shit, it didn't even occur to me," I groaned, slapping my forehead.

"It's okay. *This time.* I covered for you. I'm sitting in a diner just out of town, freezing my ass off for you. You *so* owe me," she grumbled. "Get your ass over here now."

***

I slid into the booth opposite Kass, handing her my spare jacket. She took it gratefully and slipped it on.

"You so owe me a dessert," she grumbled, still pissed.

I smiled. "Sure. Get whatever you want." I sat back, running over the night in my head. That kiss . . . I shivered as chills danced down my spine.

"Oh, I plan on it." She reached for the menu to survey her options. "So, spill."

"Huh?"

"Where were you, and who didn't you want your aunt to know you were with? And don't even *try* to lie to me," she warned, her brown eyes narrowing.

I glanced around the empty diner, fighting myself on how much to tell her. I could trust Kass, and I *needed* to tell someone. I was desperate for someone else's opinion, and there was nobody who would give it to me straighter than Kass.

"Promise this doesn't go further than you and me," I said, leaning across the booth.

She did the same. "I promise," she said, her eyes wide.

"Okay. I was with Dalton."

She looked confused, so I added "Reid."

Her eyes grew even wider. "As in . . . "

"Mr. Reid," I agreed.

"Tell me everything! Leave nothing out!" she hissed as I giggled, relieved by her reaction.

"It's hard to explain. We've had this kind of flirting thing going on for weeks now. I called him and asked him to a movie, and he said yes."

Kass's mouth dropped open.

"Kass, I feel so . . . I don't even know how to explain it. And when we kissed—"

"You kissed him?" she squealed.

I blushed and shot her a look. She immediately clamped her

mouth shut.

"It just kind of happened. Now I have no idea where I stand."

"Forget dessert. Stay at my house tonight. We need to hash this out." She grabbed my arm and steered me over to the counter. "But first, you need to pay for the five coffees I had while waiting for you."

***

Kass's bedroom was bigger than our living room at home. It was fucking huge. She had her own bathroom and balcony. Her king-sized bed barely took up any of the room. A large TV hung on the ivory-colored wall above a fireplace.

"Okay, so tell me everything," she said, wriggling out of her jeans and into a pair of gray sweatpants.

I lay down on her bed and told her everything—from the movies, to him coming over, to how I felt when I was around him. It was like a weight had been lifted off me. I'd needed to get all this out, and if not Kass, then who was I going to tell? My aunt? I snorted at the thought. I could talk to Layna about many things, but a crush on my teacher was not one of them, especially when I had just *kissed* said teacher.

Kass collapsed dramatically on the bed beside me.

"Wow," she muttered, sighing loudly. "Can you promise me

one thing?"

I turned to her expectantly.

"If, for whatever reason, this has to get out, can I be there when you tell Paige? Or better yet, can *I* tell her?" She grinned.

I burst out laughing. God, the look on Paige's face would almost be worth it.

"I told him about the betting pool," I said with a giggle.

"Ha! That's awesome. What did he say?"

"That it explained a lot," I said. "I think he was a bit bewildered with all the attention of the girls."

"Well, he's a delish young teacher. What did he expect?" She smirked. She shook her head. "Holy shit, Wrenn. This is so . . . rebellious of you. I never would've imagined you getting with a teacher."

"I haven't *gotten* with anybody. Not since Toby, anyway. And it's not like that. I really like the guy," I said quietly. The question was, did he like me?

"Toby?" asked Kass. "Was he your boyfriend back home?"

I nodded. I'd been convinced that I was in love with Toby, and looking back, I think I was. That made it so much worse when he broke up with me. When things get difficult, you don't expect someone you love to abandon you. But that's what happened. Abandoned by my family, and then by Toby.

"You never talk about your family," Kass said slowly. She eyed me as if she were not sure how I'd react.

And there it was. The questions began. It was inevitable that it would come up sometime, but the thought of telling her still made me feel sick. It wasn't that I didn't trust her, or I worried what she would think; it was more the way *I* felt when people knew that about me.

"My parents and brother were killed in an accident," I said.

Her eyes widened and she moved closer to me, her arm wrapping around my shoulders.

"My brother and mom were killed instantly, my dad died a few hours later."

"Oh God, Wrenn." She hugged me. I felt relieved that she knew. "I can't even imagine how hard that would've been."

"It was. My life before was completely different from how it is now. Toby, my boyfriend, pretty much stopped seeing me because he didn't know how to act around the girl who'd lost her family." I laughed, thinking about how awkward everyone else had acted. "I mean, *I'm* the one whose family died, yet *they* can't handle it?" I shook my head.

"And then you came here."

"Yes. Layna thought I needed to be around her. At seventeen, I could've stayed at home, but there were way too many memories…" I swallowed as tears stung my eyes. I missed them all so much.

After our deep and meaningful conversation, Kass and I watched movies and chatted about anything and everything. She was in the middle of telling me about the plans she and Trina had for the holidays when my phone beeped. She stopped midsentence and stared at me.

"Is it him?" she pressed.

I fished my phone out of my purse, my hands shaking. *It's probably just Layna. Why the hell would he text me?*

I stared at his name on my screen for a good ten seconds before opening the message.

Can I call you?

I texted back.

I'll call you. Give me five minutes.

"He wants to speak to me," I whispered, feeling sick.

Kass jumped off the bed and ran over to the balcony. "Go out here. I'll go downstairs and get us something to eat. Come down when you're finished."

I waited until she had left the room before tiptoeing out onto the balcony. The concrete was freezing against my bare feet, but I barely noticed. All I could think about was what he wanted to say to me.

I pulled up his number and pressed Call. Holding the phone against my ear, I clutched at my stomach, waiting for him to answer.

"Wrenn." *God, he sounded amazing.*

"Hey," I said, sitting down on one of the wicker lounge chairs outside the door.

"You're right. We do need to talk, so if you're still up for the movie, we'll go. I think the sooner we clear this up, the better."

My stomach flopped. The sooner we clear this up? That didn't sound promising. That sounded like a mess he wanted sorted out before anyone else saw it.

"Okay. I will see you there at seven? We can talk after the movie."

"See you then," he said, his voice soft.

***

I trudged downstairs.

Kass frowned when she saw me approaching the kitchen. "That was fast," she observed, handing me a bowl of ice cream.

I sat down at the table and nodded. "He wants to talk to me tomorrow so we can clear this up."

"Oh."

"Exactly," I agreed. I pushed the bowl away and dropped my head onto the table. "Kass, I'm an idiot."

"It's okay. Listen to what he has to say before you get yourself worked up."

"No, it's not okay. I've made a complete idiot out of myself."

"Did he kiss you back?"

"Huh?" I asked, not seeing her point.

"When you kissed him, did he kiss you back? Even for the slightest moment?"

I thought back. I'd instigated the kiss, but he had definitely reciprocated it. That was not all one-sided. There had been something between us.

"Yes," I muttered. "But that's not the point."

"What is the point? What do you want from him, Wrenn?" she asked, pointing her spoon at me.

I couldn't answer that. Did I want him to risk his career, sneaking around with me? No. But I couldn't ignore my feelings either.

Chapter Twelve

Dalton

I stared at the phone after she'd hung up, telling myself over and over that this was the right thing to do. The kiss had been amazing—*she* was amazing—but it couldn't happen. If only for the fact that I was her fucking teacher, this was wrong.

It didn't feel that way, though. When we were together it felt equal. She was as bright and mature as me. That wasn't saying much, but she wasn't your average eighteen-year-old.

Eighteen. I was only twenty-three. She was only five years younger than me, a socially acceptable age difference. The surge of anticipation that had rushed through me when I'd found out she was eighteen had shocked me. I liked Wrenn a lot, but it was only when we kissed that I realized my feelings for her extended beyond attraction. Her comment about how, had things formed differently, we could've both been in college at the same time had gotten under my skin.

She was right: I wouldn't have blinked an eye about asking out a pretty freshman.

God, those lips—so soft and smooth. And the way she'd touched my face had made me numb. My body tingled just thinking about her.

Stop! This wasn't going to happen. Tomorrow, you are going to tell her that, and then you will distance yourself from her.

Except something told me Wrenn wasn't going to be so easily swayed. And I knew it wouldn't take much pushing for me to snap. *I* have *to stop thinking about this or I'm going to go insane.*

Opening the fridge, I grabbed a soda and sat down at my computer. I logged into Skype to see if Cam was around. He wasn't, so I sent him an email.

Dude,

How's it going? Let me know when you're around and we'll Skype.

Say hi to Amy.

Dalton

I'd just clicked send when a notification buzzed through from Cam saying he was online. I clicked Call. His face popped up, and I laughed. His usual shaggy blond mop of hair was styled into place, and he wore a suit instead of his usual T-shirt and jacket.

"Nice look," I snorted.

"Yeah, well, I had an interview, then I had to do this thing for Amy. Anyway, it's not important. What's up?"

"Not much, dude. Just wanted a familiar face to chat to."

"Aww, poor Dalton's not homesick, is he?" Cam *tsked* as I laughed.

"Fuck off. I've had a hard week. This just keeps getting worse."

"That bad?" He winced, scratching his ear.

"Let's just say I'm making this much more complicated than it needs to be," I sighed. Did I tell him about Wrenn, or not? I wanted to, but something was stopping me. The less people knew about this, the better. "Anyway, things will get better. They have to, right?"

"Yeah, sure," Cam said, raising his eyebrows and not looking convinced. "So when are you back home next? We'll catch up."

"Definitely. It probably won't be until the end of my contract though."

"Sweet. Well, stay out of trouble, and you watch yourself

around those young hussies," he warned, clicking his tongue.

If only he knew.

***

After an hour of grading homework assignments, I could barely keep my eyes open. Fuck, I was tired. They could wait, because right then all I wanted to do was sleep.

I shoved everything back in my briefcase and stumbled down to the bedroom. I hung my jacket over the bedpost and peeled off my shirt, discarding it on the ground. Unbuttoning my jeans, I took them and my boxers off and climbed into bed.

It took my body a few minutes to adjust to the temperature of the freezing sheets. I lay there, almost asleep, but unable to switch my mind off. Every time I closed my eyes, I saw her. I felt myself get hard, aroused at the thought of her smile, those lips. God I could only imagine the feel of them on my…

Fuck! I rolled over, disgusted with myself. I was *not* going to jerk off while thinking about her. She was my fucking student! There was nothing I wanted more than to see where this…whatever this was, took us. But I had to be realistic.

It was never going to happen.

Chapter Thirteen

Wrenn

There were no words strong enough to explain how I was feeling as I approached the theater. He stood against the wall, staring at me, his hands shoved into the pockets of his jeans, his knee bent, foot propped up against the wall.

I'd thought long and hard about what to wear tonight, and seeing his eyes widen and his body tense, I knew the low-cut black dress and cream heels had been a great choice, even if I was freezing my ass off. I *wanted* to make him squirm inside. We both knew what he was going to say, and I was planning on testing his resolve tonight. That kiss had felt so incredible that I wasn't ready to give up on him yet.

"Wow, you look stunning," he murmured, his eyes roaming over me.

I smiled and tilted my head. I had scrubbed up pretty well. "We should go in," I replied.

He held up two tickets, and I grinned.

"I was hoping you had gotten them." I'd noticed the same young guy in the ticket booth, and the last thing I wanted was to deal with him again after the embarrassment of last night.

We walked inside. The theater was filling up. Without thinking, I grabbed his hand and led him toward the far corner of the back of the room. He jumped at my touch, but didn't resist. We sat down, his hand not letting mine go.

"Just in case someone we know is here, I thought the back corner made sense," I explained, my face flushing.

He nodded, his fingers entwining in mine, his skin so soft. "Makes sense."

I barely heard him; I was too busy focused on the way his finger was gently stroking mine. God, how was it possible that the tiniest touch was arousing me right now?

As the movie went on, I did my best to watch it, but really, all my attention was on him. It took me fifteen minutes to work up the courage to reposition my hand so mine was on top, our fingers laced. He glanced at me with a small smile.

This made me feel more confused. Was he going to end this? And if he was going to stop us before we had even really begun, why hold my hand?

I wish I had the balls to kiss him right now.

This was the perfect arrangement: a dark theater, sitting alone in the corner, holding hands—but I couldn't do it. No matter how much I ached to feel those lips against mine, I was too scared of being rejected.

Too quickly, the movie was over. We were the first people up and out of our seats, nervous about being spotted. We walked quickly to his car. He unlocked the passenger door and waited until I was safely inside before closing it.

We sat in his car in silence as I waited for him to talk. He was preparing a big speech in his head, I just *knew* it. I needed to say something now, or I'd lose my chance.

I couldn't make a bigger fool of myself, so why not go all out?

"I want to say something." I blurted it out before he could begin.

He glanced at me in surprise, but nodded.

"I like you. A lot. I understand your reservations about getting into a relationship with me, but I'm eighteen. I'm an adult, and we both have less than six weeks of school left. You're not that much older than me, and I think you like me, too. I don't expect—or even *want*—you to risk your job for me, so I'm willing to wait until school is over for the both of us before we start anything."

I took a breath, waiting for him to respond. He was staring at me with those gorgeous blue eyes, and I was melting into him.

"You're right," he finally said. "I *do* like you, Wrenn. But regardless of the fact that you're eighteen, this will always have started with you being my student. There is a balance of power thing to consider, and the ethical issues of me dating a student, or even suggesting I'd be interested in doing so when they've finished school."

I snorted. "You're worried that I'm feeling pressured by your being my teacher?" I unbuckled my seatbelt and turned to face him. Leaning over, I snaked my arm around the curve of his neck, pulling him closer to me. "Does this look like I'm feeling pressured, Dalton?"

He didn't resist, not even as my lips met his. He kissed me back, his tongue slipping inside my mouth, wrestling against my own. I jumped as I felt his hand on my hip, running down my thigh and stopping on my exposed skin.

Kissing him felt so right, like we were a perfect fit. His lips were so soft, much softer than I'd expected them to be. I ran my fingers over the soft stubble on his jaw, the feeling making my skin tingle.

"I have no idea how this can work, Wrenn. It's hard enough that I'm your teacher, but we both live on campus. That makes things nearly impossible."

"I like a challenge," I said with a smile as I caressed his face. "But if you want to wait until I graduate, I'm fine with that. I don't want you getting into trouble, nor do I want you to feel like I'm pressuring you into anything," I added, relaying his own words back to him with a hint of sarcasm.

"You act all innocent, but you're a little devil, Wrenn," he chuckled.

Grinning, I leaned over and kissed him again.

Finally, I felt like something was starting to go right in my life again.

Chapter Fourteen

Wrenn

"If you could change one thing about yourself, what would it be?"

We were lying on a blanket down at the bank of the river, staring up at the sky. It was a clear night, clear enough to make out all the twinkling stars above us. I shivered and he wrapped his arms around me, pulling the thick woolen blanket that covered us up to my chin. I giggled as he kissed me.

"Change about myself or my life?" I asked.

"Yourself. I know what you'd change about your life, Wrenn." He said it so softly I could barely hear him, but I knew he meant my family.

I sighed, and thought about his question. "I don't know. I think everything we do, we learn from, so saying I'd change one aspect of myself could potentially have changed who I am today."

I shrugged, gazing up at him. "I know I'm not perfect, but I'm happy with the person I am. I think I offer a lot as a person, and I know I still have so much to learn, but everything that happens to me, everything I am, I live and learn from."

His arms tightened around me as he kissed my forehead. "Your strength amazes me, Wrenn. Every second we spend together, you find a new way to surprise me." He kissed me, his lips in sync with mine as his fingers ran underneath my sweater. I sighed as they grazed over my breasts, my nipples instantly hardening. I wanted him so badly. These past few weeks had been nothing short of perfection. I found myself wanting to be with him more and more, and finding it harder to control my emotions went we weren't alone.

I glanced down at my phone, my heart dropping. Almost curfew. I hated leaving him.

"I have to go," I said glumly, kissing his lips one more time before I struggled to my feet.

He stood up too, his arms curling around my waist as he kissed my neck. "I wish you didn't have to go," he mumbled.

"Me too. I'll see you tomorrow." I blew him a kiss as I walked to my car, my heart heavy with sadness at leaving him. I was falling for him, there was no doubt in my mind.

I was falling hard.

***

Kass was talking in my ear about something, but I couldn't focus. All I could see was Dalton, over on the other side of the classroom, helping out another student. He laughed at something Emma had said, and my stomach churned.

Why was this getting to me so much? He was a teacher in an all-girl school, of course he had to interact with members of the opposite sex. I just didn't like having to see it.

"Wrenn? What the hell is wrong with you today?"

I jumped and turned back to Kass, who was staring at me. "Nothing," I mumbled. "What were you saying?"

"I was saying I don't know what I'm going to do for the rest of the year without you here. I'm going to miss you when you graduate."

"I'm going to miss you too. You'll be finished before know it, and we'll still see each other like all the time," I said, smiling.

She nodded and sniffed. I reached over and squeezed her hand. Kass was such a good friend, and I was so lucky to have her in my life.

***

After the final bell rang, Kass and I walked out of class, past Dalton's desk. I could feel him staring at me. Sure enough, when I turned, his eyes were on me—all over me. I smiled, and winked at him, which made him chuckle. He turned back to his desk, a smile still on his lips, and I knew he was thinking about me.

The longer this went on, the harder it was getting for both of us. When you feel so strongly for someone, you don't want to keep it a secret. You want to shout it from the rooftops. You want everyone to know what you're feeling. Hiding it feels so wrong. How can falling in love ever be a bad thing?

But it was. At least, that's what society wanted us to think. We could have the most exceptional circumstances in the world and it wouldn't make a damn difference.

He would always be my teacher, and me, his student. I just prayed he could get past that.

Chapter Fifteen

Dalton

The more time I spent with Wrenn, the more I liked her the more I liked her. Every moment I spent with her, she cemented herself a little bit more in my life. Slowly, she was beginning to unravel the walls I'd built around myself.

And that made me nervous.

I laughed to myself. The funny thing was that she could sense my anxiety about our relationship, and she thought it was all to do with the fact that I was her teacher. That couldn't be further from the truth. Honestly? The risk of losing my job—I'd risk it all in a second for her. How bad was that?

No, this ran much deeper. It killed me that it was always in the back of my mind. One test, and I'd know. One way or the other I'd know for sure. But I didn't want to know. Hell, I was angry at my own mother. Why couldn't she have lied to me? I wouldn't have known the difference. I could have lived my life not caring.

Sometimes it was best not knowing.

***

The realization hit me late one afternoon after Mom texted me, reminding me it was coming up to the anniversary of Dad's death. I couldn't do this. It *had* to stop. I had to think of Wrenn before this went any further. I could end it now. I wasn't sure I'd have the strength if I left it much longer.

Picking up my phone, I texted her, asking her to meet me down by the river. A deserted space, the river was a favorite place for us to meet, because it was so far out of the way there was no chance of us getting caught.

Sure. Give me twenty minutes xx

I grabbed my jacket and headed to my car. I couldn't think straight. All I wanted was to take her in my arms, and feel her skin against mine, and taste those sweet little lips. Fuck, she was intoxicating. Even the thought of her being close to me got me hard. Hell, thinking about her in class last week had gotten me aroused.

That's a good look.

How the hell was I going to end this and still be around her for the next few weeks? And then what? She'd made it clear she would wait for me. What excuse would I have when she was no longer my student?

I thought about telling her everything, but I didn't want pity. I didn't want her to confuse her feelings of sympathy with desire for me. Yet I hated the thought of her not wanting me at all.

The thought of her kissing some teenage boy who knew nothing about pleasing her made me want to punch the shit out of someone. The kinds of emotions I was feeling were completely new to me, and honestly, they scared me.

The drive to the river was ten minutes. She was there already. Waiting for me. Her face lit up when she saw me, her lips parting into a smile that reached those stunning green eyes. I breathed in hard as she stepped out of her car. She looked so fucking sexy. Her boots came up to her mid-calf over her tight jeans, which showed all her curves. She wore a fitted blue sweater under her jacket.

My heart raced as I stepped out of my car. She leaned in to kiss me, and I let her. I was here to break up with her, yet all I wanted to do was explore every inch of that body with my hands, my mouth, and my tongue. I laughed. *Oh, the irony.*

God, all I could smell was the sweet floral scent of her perfume. And the freshness of her skin. She waited for me to say something, her brow furrowing as she studied my face. She knew something was wrong.

"Wrenn. I can't do this to you. We need to stop this before it goes any further." There, I said it. Did I feel any better?

No. I felt like shit.

She stepped back, crossing her arms over her chest, her eyes widening. She hadn't been expecting me to say that.

"What do you mean, we can't?" she said evenly. "You didn't seem to have any problem with it the last few weeks." She was hurt. I could see it in her eyes. And I didn't blame her. It had come out of nowhere.

"I'm sorry. This . . . I can't do this." I so badly wanted to elaborate, but I couldn't.

What could I tell her? That I was so close to falling in love with her? That the last thing on my mind was the fact she was my student? I was hiding something, something so potentially life-changing—for both of us. Something she deserved to know.

But how could I tell her? How could I be responsible for breaking her heart like that? I'd rather end this now and have her think I was a weak piece of shit.

"I don't care that you're my teacher, Dalton. I don't give a damn about that." She was angry now. Her green eyes flashed as she stared me down. So much fire and passion for such a quiet girl. She knew what she wanted, and she wasn't going to give up without a fight.

"But I do," I fibbed. "My career, Wrenn. I've worked too hard to get where I am to ruin it all on . . . " My voice trailed off. The only way to do this was to convince her my career meant more to me than she did.

"On me?" she supplied. Her face hardened. "I get it. You don't want to throw your career away on some fling, right? I was just some cheap entertainment to get you through the year?" She glared at me, demanding an answer that I wouldn't give her. She nodded. "I'm surprised you didn't fuck me while you had the chance," she taunted.

I looked away. I hated seeing her this angry. "Wrenn—"

"Don't bother," she interrupted. "Obviously we're not on the same page. We never were."

She ran to her car and jumped in, roaring out of the parking lot. I threw my arms back behind my head, angry with myself. Angry with my father. Angry at the whole fucking useless world.

Wrenn was unlike any woman I'd ever met—so feisty and sure of herself. But she wasn't a woman, she was still a girl. Her being eighteen didn't make this right. She'd been through more heartache than most people go through in their whole lives, and she'd dealt with it with such maturity and dignity. But none of that changed the fact that I couldn't be with her—if anything, it magnified that fact.

It just wasn't right, and it wasn't fair to her.

She was angry now, but I knew that would melt away. And once it did, she wouldn't give in without a fight. Today I had won. But if she pushed me, I'd break; and when that happened, nothing would keep me from her.

God, I hope she respects my decision.

Chapter Sixteen

Wrenn

I was pissed.

Who was he to call all the shots? So he was scared. Big fucking deal. Grow a pair and deal with it. I'd coped with more in the last year than he ever would. I didn't need him protecting me.

The way I felt about him had gone beyond some schoolgirl crush. We connected on so many levels. But he just couldn't get past the fact that he was my teacher.

I've lost too much to let him slip away. I won't let that happen. I refuse to.

I spent the rest of Sunday watching DVDs and glancing at my phone, hoping he would call or text—anything—to tell me he had changed his mind. Layna had commented on my foul mood, which I had chalked up to my period. That stopped any further questions. Possibly the only time my period had ever come in handy.

I hated the way I was feeling. He made me feel so vulnerable, so open to getting hurt. I hated that, and right now, I hated him. I considered faking being sick so I didn't have to see him the next day, but part of me wanted to be there. I wanted to rub in his face what he was missing.

My phone beeped and I lunged at it, sighing when I saw it was only Kass. I read her message.

I'm guessing your weekend was as fun as mine *wink, wink*

I groaned and replied.

Only if you were at the dentist having teeth pulled. He ended it.

It took her less than ten seconds to call me.

"He what?" she yelled.

I held the phone away from my ear. "Ended. Finished. Over. Done," I mumbled, digging a piece of lint out from under my nail. I wasn't in the mood to talk about it, not even with her.

"Oh, Wrenn. Why? What happened?"

"I don't know. He just said it was too much and he *couldn't do it anymore*," I mimicked. I heard the downstairs door slam shut. "Look, I'll talk to you tomorrow. Someone is home."

I shuffled downstairs and saw Dan with his bike in the middle of the living room, changing the tube in the tire. He looked up and smiled as I walked in and slumped on the sofa.

"Hey kiddo."

I watched as he levered the tire off the wheel. "Layna would kill you if she knew you were doing this inside," I commented sullenly.

"That's why we're not going to tell her." He smirked, winking at me.

I smiled in spite of my mood, throwing my legs over the arm of the chair.

"You okay, Wrenn? You seem really off."

"I'll be fine. Just having a bad day, I guess."

He nodded and set down his tools. He walked over and joined me on the sofa. "Your aunt loves having you here with us. I do too," Dan said.

I nodded. They hadn't once made me feel unwelcome, and I appreciated that.

"You know, Layna always wanted children. I think that's part of why she is so passionate about her job."

"What happened?" I asked shyly. I'd always gotten along well with Dan, but these heart-to-hearts were not common. I felt in the way around him. Like I had invaded their life. Which, in a way, I had.

"Life happened. We left it too late to start trying, and by the time we found out she would never carry a child naturally, it was too late. We tried IVF. She fell pregnant twice, and lost the baby in the first trimester with both pregnancies." He smiled at me. "All I'm saying is, don't for a second underestimate how much that woman—and I—love you."

I nodded, feeling the tiniest bit better. I'd never doubted that they loved me, but I had wondered what would have happened if there had been other people who could have taken care of me.

"Thanks, Dan. I love you guys too. And I'm sorry if I don't tell you enough, but I'm so grateful for everything you've done for me."

He reached over and squeezed my hand. "You're a good kid. If you ever need to talk, I'm here, okay?"

I nodded, smiling at him.

***

At six, I made myself a sandwich and went to bed, claiming I wasn't feeling very well. I don't think either Layna or Dan believed me, but they let me go. I stripped down, pulled on my pajamas, and climbed under the covers, snuggling up to my pillow.

I thought about Dan. Had he told Layna about our talk? Probably. In fact, I hoped he had. I probably didn't express myself very well to them, and I should. I'd never been shy about telling my family I loved them, why did I find it so hard to show my aunt and uncle? Maybe I was afraid of losing them too?

That was a big part of it.

It wasn't that I couldn't let myself feel close to people, but more that I was afraid of telling them how I felt, because in the past, everyone I had loved had left me. It was like my mind contradicted my heart. Yes, you can love that person, but be careful how much emotion you show. *Or maybe I have no idea why I am the way I am.*

The latter was much more likely.

I lay in bed, thinking about how different everything was now, from then. I hated that my family had been taken away from me, but there was nothing I could do to change that. With Dalton, I could. I could sit back and accept that this was what he thought was best, or I could fight for what *I* wanted, for once.

Chapter Seventeen

Dalton

I was dreading walking into that classroom. I had no idea how I was going to get through the next forty minutes. Talk about awkward. This situation topped that list.

I finished my coffee in the teacher's lounge and rinsed out my mug, well aware the bell was about to sound. I was procrastinating, avoiding the impending situation for as long as I possibly could.

Wrenn had been really angry yesterday. It had crossed my mind that she might turn me in, but I ruled out the thought as quickly as it had appeared. She wouldn't do that, no matter how angry she felt.

Mark was next to me, talking about something. I nodded occasionally, pretending to listen, when in reality I had no idea what he was even saying. He didn't seem to notice.

"Good, we will see you tonight at eight, then. You'll like her, trust me."

My head snapped up as I realized I might've agreed to something I didn't want to. That last comment sounded an awful lot like I'd just agreed to a date.

"What?" I asked

"Julie. She's cute and really hot. I'm sure you two will hit it off." Mark waved at me as he walked off. I'd have to talk to him at lunch.

Fucking great.

***

The walk down the hall to my room felt like the longest of my life. I could see the students grouped outside the door, waiting for me. I reached the door and unlocked it. Girls whispered and giggled, but all I could focus on was *her*. Even without looking, I knew she was staring at me. I swallowed, my throat as rough as sandpaper.

The door swung open. I stood back, letting the students file in first. I met Wrenn's gaze as she and Kass walked past me. Her eyes were narrowed. She was still angry. I hated seeing her angry, but that passion hit something deep inside me, making me *feel* much more than I was ready to admit. I shut the door and walked over to my desk.

"Okay. Quiz time. Books away, just a pen out, please."

Groans filled the room, but I didn't care. Today, I wanted the least interaction with this class I could have. I handed out the quiz sheets and then sat back down at my desk, opening my laptop.

I scrolled through page after page, uninterested in everything. Clicking on my personal email, I saw I had a new message. It was from her. My hands shook as I clicked on Open. God, I felt so sneaky. I may as well have been looking at porn.

Dalton,

I understand why you ended things, but I want you to know I don't give up that easily. You know I've been through a lot, and I think you think you're sparing me more pain or whatever, but in reality all you're doing is hurting me.

My feelings for you aren't superficial. They're not going to go away because you decide what we're doing is wrong. Nor are your feelings for me.

Can we talk about this?

W xx

I glanced up, breathing heavily. She was staring at me, like she knew I was reading her email. I looked away. I was so stupid to have encouraged her feelings. It would serve me right if this blew up in my face.

I moved my fingers across the mouse pad and pressed delete on the email. I closed my laptop and pulled out a handful of half-graded papers, deciding that a boring, repetitive task was exactly what I needed right now.

The rest of the hour went quickly, and quietly. I told the students they could leave when they handed in their sheet. Before long, the room was empty—except for myself, and Wrenn.

I knew what she was doing. She should have blitzed through this. She wanted to get me alone. She wanted to test my resolve.

I stood up and cleared my throat. "Time's up."

She grabbed her bag and walked up to the desk, sliding the sheet across, her eyes not leaving mine. "Can we talk?" she asked me, sitting on the edge of my desk, her skirt riding up her creamy white thighs.

I glanced at the door. Thank God it was shut. If she tried to kiss me right now, I probably wouldn't resist. Hell, if she tried to fuck me right here on the desk I didn't think I could resist.

"Not here, Wrenn," I said, keeping my distance. If I got too close, I didn't trust myself. I wanted her that badly.

"Then where? Tonight? Meet me."

"I can't. I have a meeting," I lied. I gathered up my things and walked over to the door. "I'm sorry, Wrenn."

She held my gaze and then nodded, her lips pressed tightly together. "You know, in three weeks, you won't be my teacher anymore," she muttered sullenly. And just like that, she'd reverted back to the eighteen-year-old child she was.

"No, but I still would have been someone you trusted who abused his power. And think about it. How's it going to look? That we 'suddenly' decide to date as soon as my contract is over? Come on, Wrenn. Nobody is stupid enough to believe that bullshit." I was being harsh, but she just wasn't getting it.

"I don't give a damn what everyone thinks," she retorted, her voice rising.

"Really? Not even your aunt?"

She shut her mouth and glared at me for a moment.

"I have to go, Wrenn. This is for the best. You'll see."

***

Throwing myself down on the sofa, I groaned as I realized I'd forgotten to talk to Mark about canceling the "date." I glanced at the clock hanging on the wall above the fridge; it was already past seven.

Too late now.

I didn't have a choice. Getting up, I threw on a pair of jeans and a shirt, not taking too much care in my appearance. A quick run though my hair with my fingers and I was done. Grabbing my keys, I headed for my car, already wanting the night to be over.

***

Mark's text said to meet them outside the steakhouse in town. It was pretty busy for a Monday night. The place was as corny as you could get, with stuffed animal heads adorning the walls and the waitresses dressed up as cowgirls, but they apparently did the best steak in the county. I spotted Mark and Shelly at a booth, with them an attractive blonde woman who looked around my age.

"Hi guys," I said, sliding into the booth next to the woman who could only be Julie. She gave me a smile. She was very pretty. Her blonde hair fell down her back. She wore a black pleated skirt and an aqua-colored sweater that looked striking against her porcelain white skin.

"Julie, this is Dalton. Dalton, Julie," Mark introduced us.

"Nice to meet you," I murmured, taking her outstretched hand. She smiled at me. "And lovely to see you again, Shelly."

Shelly smiled at me, her hand casually draped over Mark's.

"So, you're a teacher too?" Julie asked.

I nodded.

"I don't know how you handle all the hormones," she chuckled. "And being so attractive, I bet all your students have crushes on you."

"Maybe one or two," I admitted awkwardly, trying to laugh off the uncomfortable weight sitting on my chest.

"I don't know what's so special about him," grumbled Mark, which earned him a smack across the ear from Shelly. "What?" he protested.

Mark was right: Julie was funny, friendly, and very attractive. She would have been perfect if I was interested in dating.

And if I wasn't already in love with someone else.

Holy shit, where did that come from? I was in love with her? Not that it changed anything. We couldn't happen. Not now, not in a month. Not ever.

***

I went through the motions of the date, from pretending to listen to asking questions to laughing when she made a joke. At one point I saw Mark and Shelly exchange a look, one that read 'this is going really well!'

By that point I was already planning on what I'd say to Mark.

I'd just come out of a long-term relationship. She'd hurt me pretty bad, and I wasn't ready to move on…Blah, blah, blah.

Glancing at my watch, I was surprised to see it was only eight. Fuck. It felt like I'd been sitting here for hours. My mind drifted to Wrenn. What was she doing right now? Probably lying down on the sofa watching a horror movie. I smiled at the thought. That was exactly where I'd rather be right now; curled up with Wrenn, watching movies while moving her hair aside and kissing her neck.

Why did my head always wander back to her?

Chapter Eighteen

Wrenn

"Come on, it'll do you good." Kass grabbed hold of my arm and dragged me inside the restaurant. The place was packed. The last thing I felt like doing was going out, but Kass had insisted. I stood next to her while she organized a table for us. I scanned the faces, hoping there wasn't anyone from school there. That was all this day needed. Then I spotted him.

You've got to be kidding me. He was on a fucking date. I studied the blonde, picking out every negative thing I could find about her, which didn't amount to much. She was pretty, well-dressed, and she laughed a lot. I hated her already.

"I can't be here," I mumbled to Kass, trying to push my way past her. She followed my gaze, her eyes nearly popping out of her head. She stopped me as I went to walk out.

"No," she said, a smile twitching on her lips. "I have an idea." She whipped out her phone and sent a text. "Can you make that a table for four please? Preferably over there." She pointed in the direction of Dalton.

What the hell was she doing? My expression must have been uneasy, because she touched my arm, her eyes softening.

"Trust me," she murmured.

We waited ten minutes—ten extremely awkward and anxiety filled minutes—before we were led to a table…right next to Dalton's. Kass gripped my arm, nudging me to move. My feet finally found their place. I followed Kass, not letting myself look in his direction.

We sat down. I forced myself to look straight ahead, but out of the corner of my eye I could see him staring at me. I turned to stare back at him, raising my eyebrow at the blonde. He looked embarrassed. I shook with anger. He fucking *should* be embarrassed.

I didn't want to be here. I wanted to be anywhere *but* here, watching him enjoy his date with the pretty blonde who *wasn't* his student.

"What are we doing, Kass?" I asked, confused. "Is this your way of torturing me?"

"Trina is on her way with her brother." She raised her eyebrows. "Her hot older brother."

"Please tell me she doesn't know," I groaned. I felt embarrassed enough without more people knowing I was in love with my teacher.

"Relax. I said there is a guy here that brushed you off; I didn't say who he was. We will say it's him." She nodded to a guy on the other side of the diner, looking all cozy with a girl. He was around our age. I began to relax.

I kept my eyes on the front entrance, waiting to spot Trina. Finally I saw her.

Fuck me. Kass wasn't kidding when she said Trina's brother was hot. He was tall, blond, with muscles in all the right places. He looked like a surfer. If my aim was to make Dalton jealous, this guy couldn't be any more perfect.

"Now play along, okay?" Kass muttered, smiling at Trina.

"Hey guys, sorry we're late." Trina leaned over and kissed Kass on the lips. The brother smirked at me. I blushed, wondering what Trina had said to him. How embarrassing was this? Imagine if he knew it was a teacher I was trying to make jealous.

"You must be Wrenn," he said, reaching for my hand. I nodded, forcing a smile. "I'm Shannon." He yanked my arm, forcing me to my feet, embracing me in a hug. Then he kissed me. It was just a peck on the lips, but I stared at him in shock.

I snuck a glance in Dalton's direction. His eyes were on Shannon, and he looked mad as hell. He looked like he wanted to kill Shannon. I giggled and draped my arm over Shannon's, and then glanced back at Dalton. He glared back at me though narrowed eyes, his face dark with anger.

It was working!

"You know, that guy's a jerk. If he can't see what a catch you are, he doesn't deserve you," Shannon murmured, staring into my eyes. His hand closed over mine, his fingers trailing up my arm. I blushed and pulled away. This guy was an ass. But he was an ass who was making Dalton more jealous than I'd seen any man, ever.

"Really? And you've figured that out in the last few minutes?" I said dryly, arching my eyebrow.

He grinned, flashing his perfect white teeth at me. I rolled my eyes and reached out, placing my hand over his. Kass winked at me, happy I was playing the game.

"I know a good thing when I see one. When you're ready to give up on these boys, come find me." He rubbed his lips together. "Come and see how a real man can treat you."

I burst out laughing and shot Kass a look. She shrugged helplessly. *Was this guy serious?* This had to be part of his act. Surely!

"Thanks, but if you're the definition of a real man, I think I'll pass."

He shrugged, his ego not bruised in the slightest. "You'll change your mind. They always do." He leaned back in his chair and smirked at me, his eyes narrowing as they ran over my body. Sweatpants and a hoodie? Yeah, I looked hot. If I'd known I was going to see Dalton, I would've dressed up.

"Hmm, maybe we should order?" I picked up my menu to hide my smile. This guy was a tool. But it was working: Dalton was furious. I could tell from the way he couldn't keep his eyes off me. I could *feel* the anger radiating from him.

I ordered fries and a steak, medium rare.

"Rare? I like a girl who knows how to eat her meat. Do you like eating meat, Wrenn?" Shannon smirked, running his tongue over his lips.

I rolled my eyes, excusing myself, then rushed off to the bathroom. I didn't need to go, I just needed to get away from this guy's ego for a moment, and regroup.

I pushed my way through the white double doors on the far side of the restaurant and made my way down to the bathroom. *Okay, Wrenn, you've got this*. I stared at my reflection as doubts began to creep into my mind. What if this didn't work? What then?

I talked big about not giving up without a fight, but really, if he wasn't interested, what choice did I have?

I walked out of the bathroom and ran into something hard. I gasped. Dalton. He grabbed my arm and yanked me into what looked like a storage room, slamming the door closed. I'd never seen him so angry.

"What are you doing, Wrenn?" he growled, his voice laced with anger. He glared at me, his eyes so dark they were almost black. The hairs on the back of my neck stood up as I wrestled my arm from his grasp.

"I'm doing the same thing as you. Having dinner," I shot back.

"You know what I mean. Who's the guy?"

I snorted. "What business is it of yours?" I asked angrily. "You made it clear that we are over. You have no say in what I do." I stared him down. "Anyway, it looks to me like you moved on pretty fast. Meeting, huh?"

"I got roped into coming here tonight. The last place I want to be is here with *her*." He said "her" like she was a disease. The familiar pang of anxiety began to stir in my stomach. Could he be telling the truth?

I stepped forward, pressing myself against him. He stared

down at me, his hands curving around my neck. When his lips met mine, my heart stopped. Everything stopped. All that mattered was him and me. The feel of him, the smell of him . . . it was like I couldn't get enough of him.

He lifted me onto his hips, pressing my back against the wall behind me. He kissed his way down my neck, his tongue rolling in soft circles over my skin. I reached out, my fingers running through his beautifully soft hair as his mouth found mine again. I moaned, grinding myself against his hips, the feel of his erection against my thigh arousing me like nothing else. I loved that I made him so hard. I wanted him, right there and then.

"Fuck, Wrenn. We can't do this here," he whispered in between kisses, his hands roaming under my shirt, cupping my breasts. Thank God he said here, because if he had knocked me back again I think I would have punched him.

"I know. I better get back or Kass will come looking for me."

He set me down, his hands running up over my back, sending shivers down my spine. "So, are you going to tell me who the guy is?"

"What?" I asked, confused.

"The punk at your table. Do I need to crunch some heads?"

I rolled my eyes as he grinned at me. "See, it's times like now you really show your age, Reid," I teased. "He's Trina's brother. I asked him here to make you jealous after I saw you with *her*."

"Well, it worked. That guy is a douche," he said darkly. "And Trina is Kass's . . . " he trailed off.

"Girlfriend," I finished, narrowing my eyes. "I know you saw them kissing at Starbucks the other night," I added, arching my eyebrow.

He flushed. "Does Kass know about you and me?" he asked, ignoring my comment. I nodded slowly as he winced. "Wrenn—"

"I had to talk to someone. And besides, she's covered for me so much with Layna. There was no way I'd have ever gotten to see you if it wasn't for her."

"Go back to your group before they send a search party," he ordered.

I jumped as he smacked me softly on the ass.

"When will I see you?" I pouted, not wanting to leave him just yet.

"I'll call you later. If we're going to do this, we need to be careful." He glanced around the storage room and sighed. "And this is not being careful. This is being stupid."

***

I giggled and read the text again.

Did I tell you how sexy you looked tonight? You really rock the sweatpants/old hoodie look.

I replied as Kass eyed me strangely. We were driving home from dinner. I hadn't told her about the bathroom incident, but she knew something was up. My mood had done a complete flip.

Gee thanks. What can I say? I was dragged out under sufferance.

"Okay, what the hell, Wrenn?" Kass finally said, my phone vibrating again. Another text.

I can't wait to see you. Just you and me. And preferably not in a closet this time.

I put my phone down and looked at Kass, who was glaring at me impatiently.

"Come on. Spill it," she whined impatiently.

"Dalton kind of followed me to the bathroom. And we kind of got it on in a storage closet."

Kass's mouth dropped open, her eyes growing wide.

"No, not that!" I giggled, realizing what she was thinking. "But if we'd been somewhere more private, that probably would've happened."

Kass squealed and hit my arm.

"Ow!" I cried, laughing.

"You little minx, so it worked! Was he completely jealous?" she demanded, smiling.

"He wanted to beat the shit out of Shannon," I admitted with a smile.

"That's so sweet," she gushed.

"It felt good seeing him so angry, Kass. Why did that feel so good?"

"Because it means he really likes you, and isn't just after sex," she replied, her tone very matter-of-fact. I giggled. Because *she* was such an expert on guys. "Are you still a virgin?"

I blushed and shook my head, not expecting her to ask me that.

"How long would you wait to sleep with him, then?"

"I don't know," I shrugged, feeling awkward even talking about it. "When it felt right, I guess. I'm not against having sex early in a relationship."

"But?"

"I feel so inexperienced next to him. Sure, he's only five years older than me, but he's probably slept with God knows how many women. What if I'm really bad?" As soon as I said it, I cringed.

Kass burst out laughing which made me feel even worse. "Wrenn, you're young and freaking as sexy as hell. I mean, *I'd* do you. You could just lie there not moving and still be a great fuck."

I rolled my eyes at her, a small part of my liking that she thought I was hot.

She's right, I guess. If he really liked me, the sex would be special regardless of how badly I sucked—no joke intended.

"Have you given head before?" she asked with a smirk.

"For your information, I've been told I'm pretty damn good at it," I said nonchalantly.

"By who? Toby, the seventeen-year-old sexpert?" she sniggered.

I glowered at her. Okay, so maybe the source of my praise wasn't that reliable, but I still knew my way around a penis.

"But seriously, that's totally gross. I could never put one of them in my mouth. Ugh." She screwed up her nose. "I much prefer vagina."

"So you've never…"

"Nope. I've had sex with a couple of guys, but not that. I much prefer the female body. I have no problem going down on a girl, but a guy? Hell, no. You couldn't pay me enough to do that shit."

"So, what's it like?" I couldn't believe what I was asking. My curiosity had gotten the better of me.

"What?" she asked, confused.

"Going down on a girl." I blushed as Kass's eyes lit up.

She giggled, loving my embarrassment. "Ha, I knew you'd ask that! It's hard to explain." She thought for a moment. "Chicks are so soft, and usually somewhat tame, and we have three different places we can orgasm. That leaves a lot of room for… exploration. Personally I think all chicks secretly want a lesbian experience, because it's so freaking sexy. Running your tongue along the opening of a vagina is one of the most erotic things I can think of…God I can't even explain. Its really something you need to try to understand."

I laughed. "Sure, I'll keep that in mind."

Chapter Nineteen

Dalton

Two more weeks.

Two more weeks and my contract would be over, Wrenn would be finished with school, and we could be together. God, how I wished it was all that easy. I wished like hell that after those final two weeks, things would be better. But the real issue was never going to go away.

Things were never that easy. Not for me. I needed to tell her. It was such an ass move, letting her fall in love with me without letting her know the truth. Especially after everything she'd gone through. She deserved the best. And maybe I could give her that. Maybe I couldn't.

I sighed and scrolled through the job listings in front of me. Layna had hinted that there might be another contract opening up for next year. Somehow I doubted that offer would still be on the table once she found out I'd been sneaking around with her niece.

***

It was Friday evening. I'd just sent Wrenn a text to arrange where we were going to meet the next day. I wanted to do something special for her, so I had booked a cabin by Forest Lake, two hours north—far enough away so we could completely relax and enjoy each other. Seeing her with that dick in the restaurant had made me realize that I couldn't just push my feelings aside.

The sight of her with another guy had made me more angry and frustrated than I'd ever been. Following her to the bathroom and dragging her into that storage room? That was stupid. Anyone could have seen us, but the need to have her, to touch her, was far stronger than the warning bells going off in my head.

My phone beeped on the coffee table. I reached over for it.

Sounds wonderful. Can't wait to see you.

I smiled and texted back.

I wish you were here right now. Some of the things I want to do to you . . .

She replied right away.

Really? I'd like to know exactly what you want to do to me . .

I chuckled, kicking off my shoes and lying back on the sofa as

I texted back.

I'm not texting you that. You'll have to wait, and maybe someday you'll find out.

I waited for her to reply. Ten minutes passed, and no response. I'd all but given up when there was a soft knock on the door. I jumped up. Who the hell would be knocking on my door at ten at night? Unlocking the latch, I opened the door, my mouth dropping open.

Wrenn. My beautiful, sexy Wrenn. My gaze traveled down over her low-cut sweater and tight jeans that hugged her curves. She smiled at me. I swallowed, my mouth so dry.

"Are you going to let me in before or after we get caught?" she whispered.

I flushed and opened the door wide enough for her to squeeze through. "What are you doing here?" I asked her. "And why aren't you wearing a jacket? You must be freezing!"

She laughed. "I'm fine." Her green eyes narrowed. "So, we were talking about what you wanted to do to me?"

I laughed, my arms finding their way around her waist. Having her there, inside my apartment, was such a bad idea, but I couldn't resist that smile, or the way those eyes sparkled at me. I reached up, my hand cradling her face, and tilted her lips to meet mine.

"You came here to find out what I want to do to you?" I laughed, my lips seeking hers.

She grinned and nodded.

"Then I'm not going to tell you. I'll show you."

"I like the sound of that," she whispered.

I lifted her arms until they were resting on my neck, my fingers gently running under her sweater, over her soft skin. She breathed in heavily. My lips melted against hers as my tongue slipped into her mouth, curling around her own. She tasted so amazingly sweet that I felt myself harden as I thought about my mouth touching other parts of her body.

I kissed her cheek, then her jaw, finally running my tongue down her neck. She gasped, her grip on my neck tightening.

"Your skin is so soft," I whispered, kissing the corner of her mouth. My hand ran over the outside of her sweater, resting against the hem at the bottom. She smiled, letting me know this was okay. The last thing I wanted to do was rush her, but I needed to feel her body against mine.

I lifted the sweater over her head, sliding it from her arms.

My God. She wore a black bra, her breasts pushed up, creating the most glorious cleavage. My fingers trailed over the softness of her breasts. I leaned down and kissed them as her hands entwined in my hair. I tugged down the bra, exposing her hard nipples. She gasped as my mouth enclosed over one, then the other, sucking and circling it with my tongue.

"That feels amazing," she mumbled, her eyes closed. As I watched her, I could feel myself harden. *Fuck, she looks so beautiful.* I backed over to the sofa and sat down, pulling her down with me. She giggled as she collapsed on top of me, the sound of her laughter making me smile. Working her shirt down her arms, I unclasped her bra, letting both fall to the floor.

She straddled me, her bare chest almost too much for me to take in, my erection painful against the restraint of my jeans. She knew it, too. With a little gleam in her eye she ground herself against my cock, as if loving the power she had over me.

I lifted my shirt off and pulled her into me, our skin touching. I licked her neck as her erect nipples teased the skin of my chest.

"You're so fucking amazing," I growled, my hand caught in her hair at the base of her head. I forced her toward me, my mouth desperate to explore hers. As our lips touched it was like the whole world stopped; all I cared about was her and making her happy. The pounding in my chest echoed through my ears as our tongues mingled.

God, I could taste you all night. My hands roamed her curves, running over her breasts, squeezing and teasing. I so badly wanted to feel myself inside her, but I didn't want to rush this. I pulled away and she looked at me, panting softly, her cheeks red. I smiled and smoothed her wild hair, memorizing everything about her.

She stared at me as I reached out and traced my fingers around her nipple. This was turning me on so much. Almost as though she'd read my mind, she slipped off my knee and onto the floor.

My heart rate increased. *Was she really about to do this?* I slid my ass further down the sofa as she undid my belt, then the buttons on my jeans. She reached inside my boxers carefully, as if she was handling a venomous snake. The thought made me smile.

"What's so funny?" she asked, narrowing her eyes.

"Nothing. You look kind of terrified," I said.

She blushed.

Fuck, this girl was perfect.

"I'm nervous," she admitted. "I mean, I know what I'm doing, but you're so much more experienced than me…I don't want to make a fool of myself."

I shook my head and laughed. "Do you see how aroused you make me? I'll be lucky if I can last more than ten seconds with your mouth on me. Trust me, whatever you do will be the best I've ever had."

Her eyes narrowed as she took me in her hand. Oh God. Slowly she worked her fist up and down the length of my shaft. She bent down, curling her tongue around the tip of my cock, staring up at me with those big green eyes, which were framed by long dark lashes.

"Ohh," I groaned as I watched myself disappear into her open mouth, her tongue tickling and stroking me as her lips moved along my length. Fuck, God this is so fucking… My train of thought abandoned me as I arched my back, silently willing her to suck me harder and faster. I stroked her hair, my gaze burning into hers.

Then I couldn't hold it off any longer as my cock began to throb. She sucked me hard, every motion pushing me closer to the edge until I finally jumped.

"Oh my fucking hell shit fuuuck…" I groaned again as I released into her mouth, my body jerking, unable to handle her touch but demanding it all the same.

She wiped her mouth and smiled shyly at me. "Was that okay?"

"Okay? That was mind-blowing. Fucking *hell*, Wrenn. That

was…I don't even have words." I lay back on the sofa, not capable of sitting up.

She got to her feet and curled up on top of me, her head resting on my chest. I kissed her hair, breathing in the coconutty scent of her shampoo, still unable to comprehend what had just happened.

An hour later we were still on the sofa. The TV was on, but neither of us were paying attention to it. I tickled her back as she smiled, her eyes closed. I studied her face. She was so pretty. I felt like that was all I ever said, but I couldn't get over how beautiful she was.

"Mmm, that's nice," she mumbled as I stroked her neck.

"I like making you feel good," I said, breathing in the scent of her perfume.

She smiled again, opening one eye to look at me. "I always feel good when I'm around you. I feel relaxed and excited at the same time. I feel safe and scared. You bring out everything in me."

"Same," I muttered, kissing her head. "I've never felt so close to anyone before. I don't know what it is with you, but I feel connected to you. Like I was meant to meet you." I made a face. "God, I sound like such a girl."

She laughed and shook her head. "I dunno, Mr. Reid, I like

this sensitive side of you." She grinned at me, her chin resting on my chest, her fingers entwined in mine.

"Yeah, well don't tell anyone. My reputation would be ruined."

She rolled her eyes. "Who am I going to tell? My aunt?"

I slapped her ass. "Not funny. *So* not funny. Are you looking forward to tomorrow?"

She nodded. "But I wish you'd tell me where exactly it is we're going."

"I want to surprise you," I said, kissing her forehead. She narrowed her eyes at me and smiled. "Trust me, you'll love it."

"So long as I get to spend the night with you, I'm happy." She sighed. "I better get back. I don't think leaving your room after sunrise would be a smart idea." She grinned and climbed off me.

I watched her as she put on her bra and then her sweater, the delicate fabric flowing down over her breasts, covering her stomach. She turned back to me, climbing back over me until she was straddling me, her dark hair falling over her face and my own.

"Thought you were leaving," I said softly.

"I just wanted to give you something."

"Yeah?" I said. Waiting. Watching. Heart pounding. Mouth dry.

She leaned down, her lips crushing against mine as her hands ran over my bare chest.

"If you don't go now, I'm going to take you down to my room and fuck you senseless," I mumbled, my hands moving over her bra.

"I wouldn't complain," she said, laughing.

"Go," I growled, narrowing my eyes at her.

She laughed and stood up. Reaching underneath her hair, she flipped it out from inside of her sweater, sending it cascading down her back like a chocolate waterfall.

"See you tomorrow." She smiled, slipping on her pumps.

I watched her leave, a smile on my face, thinking about how incredible this woman was.

Chapter Twenty

Dalton

I picked Wrenn up from Kass's house just after eight on Saturday morning. Neither of us had gotten much sleep the night before, but we were both so keen to spend more time together that it didn't matter.

She slid into my car, a little smile playing on her lips as she moved closer to kiss me. The scent of her perfume, sweet and musky, engulfed me.

"Hey," I murmured, not taking my eyes off her.

"Hey," she said back. She reached up to touch my face, her fingers running gently over my stubble. "I missed you. And yes, I realize I saw you a couple of hours ago." She giggled.

"Yeah, well I missed you too." I reached over and placed my hand on her thigh as I steered the car out onto the road. "Sleep well?"

"Not so much," she said. "So, where are we going, anyway?"

"You'll see," I replied mysteriously.

"God, I hope there's a hot tub," she said, stretching her legs out.

"Really?" I replied, amused.

"You don't understand how stressful senior year is, especially when you're having an affair with the teacher."

"Oh, so that's what this is?" I said, raising my eyebrows. She blushed, and I laughed. "You're so easy to mess with."

She narrowed her eyes at me, but her face was smiling.

"I'm looking forward to spending some time with you. I mean, I know we're always together, but this is different. This doesn't feel sneaky, or wrong." She stretched out her long legs, my eyes drawn to them like a magnet. "I want tonight to be special."

I knew right away where she was going with that, and I was determined not to pressure her, no matter how badly I wanted her. I should've been more at odds with myself. The idea of sleeping with a student should've been tearing me up inside, much more than it was. But it wasn't. I was worried about my job, and how all of this could affect her, but all of my reservations about taking us further had little to do with my feelings about being her teacher and everything to do with the rest of my life.

"I want this to be special too, Wrenn. But I'm not going to rush you. I want you to be ready, even if that means waiting a month, or a year," I mumbled. She turned to me, her expression one of surprise.

"Dalton . . . I'm not a virgin," she said quietly.

"I don't care about that, Wrenn. This isn't about that; this is about *you*. I want you to want me. I want you to *need* me. And no, I'm not about to burst into a song," I said wryly. She laughed, her face lighting up at my joke.

"I think you underestimate just how much I do need you, Dalton. Am I nervous about sleeping with you? Yes, but it has nothing to do with anything, other than the fact that I *really* like you. If it's too much for me, I'll tell you. I promise."

She looked out the window at the lines of trees we were passing. She shivered, and I moved the heating up to two, and then put my hand back on her thigh.

"So, not long until you're a free man, Mr. Reid. What are your plans after your contract finishes?" She asked, changing the subject.

"Well, that depends on a few things," I said, running my hand over her thigh.

"Like what?" she pressed. She leaned her head back against the headrest, facing me, waiting for my answer.

"I guess it depends on what I get offered next. Whether I still want to teach. What you're up to . . . " Why was my heart racing? Talking about the future scared the shit out of me, but talking about a future with Wrenn was almost unbearable. "If we're together, and you're in Boston, then that's where I'll be, too."

She smiled at me and wrapped her hand over mine, and the feel of our skin touching was incredible. She stared at me for a minute, as though a thought was forming in her head.

"Do you think we can do this? I mean, actually make it work?" she asked quietly.

"Why not? People form relationships all the time. Why not us?" I shrugged.

I sounded so sure of myself, so sure of us. What I didn't admit was that I'd asked myself that same question. What if, after all this, we just didn't work? I squeezed her hand again.

"I can't tell you how this is going to turn out, Wrenn. All I can do is promise that I will do my best to make this work, if that's what we decide we want."

She nodded, her eyes meeting mine. "I think I'm already past making that decision," she said, her voice soft.

***

I pulled into the cobblestoned driveway of the cabin, the movement waking Wrenn up. She gazed out of the window in confusion, as if she'd completely forgotten where she was. She glanced at me, blinking a few times, then back at the log cabin that was our home for the night.

I'd gone all out, wanting to make this special. I couldn't wait to see her face when she saw how beautiful it was inside.

We got out of the car, the fresh country smell almost overwhelming.

"This is beautiful." She turned slowly, taking in the breathtaking views of Forest Lake and its surroundings.

"Wait until you see inside." I grabbed her hand and walked up the path to the front balcony. Using the key that had been left for us, I opened the lock, swinging open the door. Wrenn went in first, and I followed her.

"Holy shit. This place is amazing," she squeaked.

I grinned. For the amount I was paying, it had fucking better be. One night had almost cost me the equivalent of one week's pay.

I walked into the living area where Wrenn was standing. Okay. This was pretty nice. The open space made it feel much bigger than it actually was. The bedroom was off to the left, with the bathroom. A huge balcony wrapped around the right side of the cottage. Floor-to-ceiling windows separated the living area from the balcony.

"Holy shit, a hot tub! A freaking hot tub!" I jumped as Wrenn started squealing. She threw her arms around my neck, and I couldn't help but chuckle. I saw glimpses of her youth in moments like this. She pressed her lips against mine, her hands working their way under my jacket and shirt, and onto the bare skin of my back.

"Fuck, your hands are freezing!" I gasped, trying to pull away from her.

She laughed and held onto me, refusing to let me get away until I could no longer feel the cold in her.

I kissed her again; just having her so close was making me hard. I grabbed her hand and lifted her into my arms. She laughed as I carried her into the living room and threw her onto the big three-seater suede sofa.

"I'm going to make you a hot cocoa, then I'm going to cook you dinner."

"You cook?" she asked, impressed.

I nodded proudly. I wasn't the world's greatest cook, but I

could throw a decent meal together.

"How about we both cook?" she asked.

"If you insist," I replied. "I will be back."

I grabbed our bags and put them in the bedroom, throwing my wallet and phone on the nightstand. Back in the kitchen, I heated up a pot of milk, and then added the cocoa and sugar, stirring it until it dissolved. I poured it into the two mugs I'd gotten out and added a few marshmallows. I carried the steaming hot drinks back to the living room along with a bag of cookies.

"Thanks," she smiled, taking the mug with both hands. She brought it to her lips and took a sip, her lips parting into a grin. "Perfect."

"So, what did you tell your aunt about where you are?" I asked.

"With Kass. She and Trina have gone away. Layna thinks I'm with them." She smiled gleefully as she took another sip of cocoa.

"Are you hungry?" I asked her.

She nodded. "Starving."

"Come on then."

We went into the kitchen. She walked around the counter and

sat down on one of the bar stools, her hands flat out in front of her. "What are we having?"

"Spaghetti à la Reid," I said proudly.

"Can you elaborate on that?" she grinned, raising her eyebrows.

"Sure. It's spaghetti, onion, garlic, tomato, basil, and my secret ingredient—anchovies."

"Ugh. No way!" she screwed her nose up in disgust. "Sorry, but I draw the line at those fishy little monsters."

"You can't even taste it once it's dissolved into the sauce," I protested.

She shook her head adamantly.

"Fine. I'll omit the anchovies in yours." I begrudgingly agreed.

I placed a cutting board, an onion, and a clove of garlic in front of her and handed her a knife.

"Finely diced?" she asked. I nodded. While she did that, I put a pot of water on the stove to boil. Heating the frying pan, I splashed in some olive oil and added the very nicely diced onion and garlic, my mouth salivating at the smell filling the air.

"That's a lot of garlic," she grinned.

"What, now you don't like garlic?" I shot back.

"No," she giggled, "I love it, I'm just cautious about garlic breath. I was planning on doing a lot of kissing later."

"Why wait till then?" I leaned across the counter, kissing her lips. "Besides, we'll both have garlic breath, so it won't really matter." I threw in the tomatoes, some basil, salt and pepper, and then turned the heat down to a simmer. Next, I added the spaghetti to the boiling water, with a sprinkling of salt.

"You look like you're made for the kitchen," she smiled.

"I helped Mom out a lot with cooking and cleaning and things, so I'm pretty domesticated."

"Mmm. Very sexy," she laughed, her eyes twinkling at me.

I narrowed my eyes, not quite sure if she was messing with me or not.

"So, you're close to your mom?" I saw her eyes drop and instantly felt bad.

"Yeah, I am. Were you close to yours?" I asked softly.

"Yeah. I mean, we fought. I'm a teenage girl—fighting with your mom is normal—but she was also my best friend. I could talk to her about anything, you know?" She smiled in spite of herself. "Well, maybe not everything. I probably wouldn't be telling her about you."

"Yeah, that probably wouldn't go down so well," I winced. "Is Layna your only extended family?"

"Yeah. My grandparents died when I was little, and Dad had no siblings. I'm lucky to have her though. She's been so supportive. Besides, there are people worse off than me. I had a wonderful family for a short time. That was better than not having them at all." She shrugged as if it made perfect sense.

Again, she had amazed me. How can you lose so much and still remain so strong? How the hell can she be so positive? She had this way of making me feel very self-absorbed. Thinking about my life and the things I had no control over consumed me. Here was a girl who had lost everything and was still able to see the good in things.

I stirred the sauce, tasting it to see if it was ready. *Almost perfect.* All that was missing were the anchovies. The spaghetti was ready, so I strained it and then divided it into the two bowls. Over the top of one I spooned the sauce. Then I broke a few anchovies into the pan and stirred it until they had dissolved.

"Try this," I said, after I'd poured the sauce over mine. She made a face. "Just do it," I said with a laugh.

She sighed but obliged, curling a few strands of pasta around her fork before lifting it to her mouth. Her eyes lit up.

"Holy shit, that's really good," she muttered, shocked. She went back in for another forkful. I sniggered, pulling her plate back over to me.

"Have that. I'll have this one."

"Are you sure?"

"Yes," I grumbled. "Maybe you'll listen to me next time?"

"Probably not." She grinned and I laughed. At least she was honest.

***

After dinner, we talked. The conversation just flowed. I felt like we could sit there for hours and never run out of topics. I loved that she had her own opinions on things. She would argue if she didn't agree, and she was passionate about her beliefs.

"So…I might go try out that hot tub." She smiled at me mischievously.

"Really?" I murmured, stretching my arms behind my head.

She turned, stretching her leg over mine until she was sitting on my lap. Wow. She lifted her sweater over her head, dropping it on the floor. My hand found its way to her chest, my fingers releasing her breasts from the cups of her pale pink bra.

Leaning forward, I took a nipple in my mouth, flicking it with my tongue until it sat erect. She cried out as my mouth closed over her other one, my hands resting on the arch of her back.

"Maybe I'll join you in the hot tub," I murmured, kissing my way up her neck.

She cupped my face, her lips pressing against mine as my cock began to spring to life.

I stood up and hoisted her onto my hips. She kissed my neck, undoing my shirt as I carried her out to the enclosed deck, to the hot tub. Shrugging my shirt off, I set her down and kneeled in front of her. She giggled as I undid her jeans and began shimmying them down her milky white thighs. In awe of the beauty that stood before me, I kissed the edge of her pink thong as she stepped out of her jeans.

"After you," I said, gesturing to the bubbling, steamy hot water.

She gingerly stepped over the ledge, collapsing down into the water. "Ooh this is fantastic," she grinned, her eyes oozing happiness.

Unbuckling my jeans, I shuffled them off and stepped into the water. It was hot—hotter than I was expecting—but against the coolness of the night, it felt good. Falling into the water, I pulled Wrenn onto my lap, my erection very obvious.

"Someone's excited," she mumbled, kissing me.

"I'm always excited around you, Wrenn. It's so hard not to show that when we're not alone, but you always have me worked up."

"Really?" she said, draping her arms around my neck. "Tell me, what is it about me that winds you up, Mr. Reid?"

Where did I start? Everything about her excited me, from her smoldering eyes to the way she laughed. I reached around and unhooked her bra, sliding it off her shoulders. I kissed her cheek, then her jaw, slowly sucking my way down her neck to her perky, round breasts.

"Everything," I murmured, my tongue rolling over her nipple. "There is nothing about you that doesn't excite me. You make me feel alive."

She pushed my head up to meet her lips, kissing me deeply, tasting me, grinding her hips against my erection. *God, what is she doing to me?*

I couldn't stand this anymore. I couldn't have her so close to me and not be inside her. Standing up, I stepped out of the tub, holding out my hand. She took it, her brows furrowed in confusion.

After she stepped out, I lifted her into my arms and carried her through to the bedroom.

"What are you doing?" she giggled, her fingers stroking the back of my neck.

"What do you think I'm doing?" I growled, throwing her wet body down on the bed. She laughed as I climbed on top of her, my hands exploring her breasts. She moaned as I squeezed her nipple. I loved the way it hardened at my touch. God, I loved everything about her.

"Are you okay with this?" I muttered, stroking her skin. She nodded, lifting her head up to kiss me.

My fingers ran down the curves of her body, reaching the band of her lace thong. I looped my fingers around it, pulling it down, exposing her perfectly groomed pussy. She lifted her hips, allowing me to slide the thong down her legs and over her feet.

"You're fucking beautiful," I muttered as my fingers stroked her inner thigh. She parted her legs and whimpered, her arm curving around my back.

I so badly wanted to feel myself inside her—but more than that, I wanted to take my time. I pulled her close to me, kissing her stomach and slowly trailing upwards, over her breasts, to her neck. She whimpered as my finger circled the outside of her wetness, while my lips found their way back to her mouth.

Her lips caressed mine, biting and teasing me, just as I was doing to her. I kissed along her jawline, down over her neck, to her breast. Her nipple was hard as I curled my tongue around it, sucking gently, arousing her to no end. She gasped as I slid a finger inside her, another massaging her clit.

She moaned, bucking her hips, trying to push my finger further inside. I chuckled, and kissed her neck as I thrust my finger inside of her again. She was so wet, and so ready. I slid another finger inside her, moving them in and out quickly. He breathing began to shallow as she clenched her hips, locking my fingers inside of her.

"Oh, oh God, oh yes, yes, yes!" She arched her back, her hand clutching at the sheets, squeezing them in her tight grip as she rode the climax. "Stop, oh God," she cried. I chuckled, pulling my hand away, kissing her.

God I need her.

I was as hard as fuck as I lowered my boxers, kicking them off my legs. She smiled, her hand closing around my length, moving her fist in a steady rhythm up and down my shaft.

Holy shit, that feels good.

She sat up and positioned herself over me until my erection

pressed at her entrance, teasing me. I fumbled through my wallet and retrieved a condom. Tearing it open, I quickly rolled it on before laying back, my hands on her hips.

Her eyes stayed on mine as she lowered herself onto me, her tight, wet pussy milking my cock. She began to rock back and forth, her breasts bouncing softly against the movement.

I rolled over so she was under me and I was on top, her legs wrapping around my waist. My fingers brushed the edge of her hairline tenderly as I stared into those eyes. I thrust myself further inside of her as our lips found each other.

She is fucking amazing.

I moved myself inside her, every thrust bringing with it another wave of emotion. Her pussy was so tight, and so wet for me. I groaned, my length sliding in and out of her.

My movements sped up, the feel of my cock inside her almost too much to handle. My God. I wanted the feeling to last forever. There was something so fucking amazing about the build of that first orgasm, my first time inside of her.

I gripped her neck, my body tensing as I began to peak. My throbbing cock felt like it was going to explode at any second. Finally, I released, my load shooting inside her, my body jerking, unable to handle how sensitive she made me.

I kissed her, my lips hitting hers with such passion. Still inside her, I held her in my arms, not wanting the moment to end.

"That was…I don't even know," she sighed. I chuckled, confident from her dreamy smile that she was satisfied.

"You're pretty spectacular," I whispered. I rolled onto my side, bringing her into my embrace. We lay there, her back against my chest, until we fell asleep.

I felt like the luckiest guy on earth.

Chapter Twenty-One

Dalton

I was in the classroom early on Monday morning, mainly because I wanted to get my head in the right space before Wrenn arrived. It was hard not to spend the entire period staring at her. The weekend had been perfect.; it could not have been any more special. Now, just like that, it was back to reality. Back to pretending she was just my student.

I knew how important it was to keep us a secret, but it was getting harder and harder for me not to show my feelings for her around others. When she spoke, I wanted to listen. I wanted to touch her face, and smile when she laughed. God, I could spend all day staring at those beautiful blood-red lips. And that dark hair, so dark it made her eyes pop.

"Mr. Reid?"

I looked up and saw Paige walking into the room.

"Paige. What can I do for you?" I asked her, trying to keep the annoyance out of my voice. I sat back in my chair as Paige perched herself on the edge of my desk, one leg over the other, her skirt riding dangerously high. "I'd prefer you sit in the chair if you have something you need to discuss with me." I gestured to the seat that was safely on the other side of my desk.

She narrowed her eyes but obliged, jumping off my desk and walking around to the chair. "I was hoping I could arrange some one on one time with you?" She raised her eyebrow, her lips forming a smile as she held my gaze.

"One on one time?" I repeated.

"You know. *Tutoring*." There was no other way to interpret the tone of her voice. She may as well have put tutoring in air quotes. "I hear you offer tutoring to some of your students." Her eyes twinkled at me as she smiled.

"Ms. Warner," I began stiffly, "if you're suggesting what I think you are suggesting, I'll have no choice but to report this."

"Come on, Mr. Reid. I'm almost eighteen. You're not that much older than me. All I'm suggesting is that we have a little fun. Nobody else needs to know."

I wanted to laugh in her face. Did she honestly not get it? Even if I weren't her teacher, I'd have no interest in "getting" with her. Ever.

"Ms. Warner, please take your seat. And if you bring this up again, I will report you."

Her face went red. She stood up, narrowing her eyes at me.

At that moment, students began to file into the classroom. Paige turned abruptly and walked over to her desk. She slumped down, still glaring at me. The look in her eyes made me uneasy. I didn't doubt that if she wanted to, that girl could stir up a shitload of trouble.

Trying to forget Paige's proposition, trying not to pay too much attention to Wrenn, all the while trying to teach a class, was impossible. Both girls were staring at me, Paige with a scowl and Wrenn . . . well, she just looked at me with the same longing she always did.

"Paige, can you please read from the top of chapter twelve."

He eyes narrowed, but then she dropped her gaze to her textbook and began to read. I sighed, relieved. *A few minutes without her glaring at me*. A few minutes where I could sneak a glance at Wrenn, and maybe even a smile.

This was insane. I was losing control. All I could think about was Wrenn, to the point where it was interfering with the rest of my life.

ALWAYS YOU

This girl was getting under my skin— and I loved it.

Chapter Twenty-Two

Wrenn

I walked across the grounds over to the house, feeling great. Things were going really good. I felt like everything was beginning to fall into place, and I could see the end. Paige had even stopped making my life hard.

In less than two weeks I would be free of this place forever. Less than two more weeks and I could go out in public with my boyfriend. We could do normal, *couple* things. I felt my phone vibrate in my pocket. It was Dalton.

Can I see you? I miss your pretty little face.

I giggled as I replied.

You saw my pretty little face yesterday in class.

He replied right back.

That's true, but there are things I want to do to you that

would get me fired if I did them to you in the classroom.

"Hey, slut."

I turned around and glared at Paige, who stood behind me, scowling, with one hand resting on her hip. So much for her leaving me alone.

"What do you want, Paige?" I sighed. I was not in the mood for this. Not today.

"I just wanted to talk. For old times' sake."

I snorted. What the hell was she talking about? I rolled my eyes and adjusted the bag of books over my shoulder, waiting impatiently for her to get to the point.

"Leave me alone, Paige. You know the best thing about leaving this place in two weeks' time? Never having to see your skanky little face again." I turned and began walking away.

She sniggered behind me. "Really? I would've put money on it being you being able to fuck your boyfriend without him at risk of losing his job."

What? I froze, positive I'd misheard.

There was no way in hell she knew. It just wasn't possible. Paige walked slowly around me until her eyes were level with mine. "Yeah, that's right. I figured it out. And your reaction just now? That confirmed it for me."

"What do you want?" I said through gritted teeth.

She laughed. "Nothing you can give me, that's for sure," she smirked. "I'll be in touch."

I watched her walk away.

"Oh, and Wrenn?" she said sweetly. "Tell that boyfriend of yours he could've done *so* much better than you."

***

After practically running home and locking myself in my bedroom, I called Dalton.

"Hey." He sounded happy to hear from me.

"Paige knows. She knows about us." I sank down onto my bed, covering my face with my hand. "What the hell are we going to do?"

"What did she say?" Dalton's voice was flat.

I recounted our conversation, leaving out the last bit where she'd said he could do better.

"I knew it. She practically propositioned me after class today."

Huh? She what?

That fucking bitch. Suddenly, all I felt was anger.

"I'm sorry Dalton, I know how bad this will be for you—"

"Hey," he cut in. "If she tells, she tells. It doesn't change how I feel about you, okay? And honestly? I'm not that worried. I think the last thing Paige would want is for her classmates to think of her as a rat."

I wished I was that convinced.

"Maybe we should lay low for a few days," I muttered, my head a scramble of conflicting thoughts. The idea of not seeing him was torture, but this was turning into a mess.

"I can't not see you," he murmured. "Come over tonight. Spend the night with me." His voice dropped low and husky. How could I say no when he sounded so damn sexy?

"Okay," I sighed. "I just can't say no to you."

Chapter Twenty-Three

Dalton

I hadn't slept at all. I'd spent the whole night with her in my arms, watching her sleep. She looked so peaceful, so relaxed. So innocent, as though nothing in the world could touch her. Thoughts invaded my head, all about her and what she was doing to me. It was like I was scared to go to sleep just in case I woke up and all this was only a dream.

Just before five, I woke her. The sun was coming up, and I knew if we left it any longer the risk of us getting caught would increase. She stirred, but didn't rouse. I smiled and leaned over to her, my lips touching hers. This time she smiled, her eyes opening and gazing up at me.

"This is a nice way to wake up," she mumbled, stretching her body. I ran my hand under the covers, gently stroking her breast. She smiled again, lifting her mouth up to meet mine.

"It's getting light outside. You'd better go," I said, not

bothering to hide my disappointment. If I could've held her captive in my bed all day, I would have.

"Yeah, I know," she grumbled, fishing around for her clothes. "I can't wait until I don't have to sneak off. I just want to be able to lie in bed with you."

"I know," I muttered. I reached for her arm, pulling her back down onto the mattress.

She laughed, letting herself fall over me—her hair over my face, her lips slammed against mine; I couldn't get enough of her.

Hours, days together—none of it was enough. A lifetime with her wouldn't be enough.

She struggled away from me, laughing. Her cheeks flushed red. Her green eyes narrowed at me as she put enough distance between us so that I couldn't reach out to her again. I shook my head and chuckled, watching her dress. Fuck, she was so sexy. Standing there in her mismatched panties and bra, trying to figure out what way around her top went—every part of me ached for her.

She bit her lip and smiled at me as she wriggled into her jeans. With one last kiss, she was gone. Out the door, and into the night. I fell back to sleep, imagining she was still there with me.

***

Friday's classes went by quickly. After work, I went home, having a few hours to spare before I was due at Layna's. I'd missed the last couple of dinners having been with Wrenn, and my non-appearance hadn't gone unnoticed. Layna had joked that if I weren't at this one, she'd come looking for me. I didn't doubt that she would.

I had a theory that Mom had been speaking to her. Mom was worried about me, but then again, she was always worried about me. Especially since Dad had died. Mom spent nearly all her time invested in taking care of me and making sure I was okay.

I dug out my phone and dialed Mom. I felt bad that it had been a few days since I'd spoken to her. Knowing how much she worried, I should have made more of an effort. She answered on the fourth ring.

"Hey honey," she said warmly.

I closed my eyes and pictured her smile. "Hey, Mom. How are you?"

"Good. Busy, but good. How are you, how's work?" she asked.

"Fine. Almost over, and then I'll be back home."

"And I can't wait," she replied. "Have you applied for any jobs for next year?"

"Not really. I was thinking of doing my elementary certificate. I don't think I'm cut out for teaching teenagers." I chuckled.

"I was always surprised that you went high school instead of elementary," Mom agreed. "If that's what you want, then do it."

"Yeah. Maybe I will."

After ending the call with Mom, I thought more about the next year. The more I thought, the more I realized that's what I wanted to do. I grabbed my laptop and navigated my way to Boston University's courses website.

Fuck it. I'll do it. I clicked Apply Now, and spent the next twenty minutes completing my application for the post-graduate course that was due to start midyear. It felt good, like I had a plan. I knew where I was heading for once.

Just as I was about to shut my computer down, an email from Cam popped up.

Hey man,

I got a freaking job! Finally! It's a year-long contract for next year in a decent public school in Farisbrook. Guess I'm growing up, huh? Time to start acting responsibly, and curb the drinking and late nights. Good thing I have a few months to clean up my act ;)

How's life in private schoolgirl wonderland? Still hating it? Ha! You should put in for a job back here.

Keep in touch man.

Cam

I chuckled at the thought of Cam as a full-time teacher. Early mornings and paperwork were not his strong points. I often wondered if he realized how much work went into teaching, or if he'd chosen it because of the excessive holidays. Either way, he was about to find out.

Congrats, man, that is fantastic! What will you be teaching?

Things here are the same. Only two weeks left, and I'm free. Not sure what's next for me. Thinking about going back to college and getting my elementary degree. Less hormones to worry about.

What are you doing over break? We should catch up. There is someone I'd like you to meet.

I pressed Send, and then second-guessed the last sentence of my email. Cam knew me well enough to know I didn't do relationships. He didn't know why, but from my countless one-nighters throughout college, he knew me bringing someone home would be a big, big thing, because it was something I'd never done.

***

Just as I was about to leave, I picked up my phone and saw there was a text from Wrenn.

When you see me tonight, just know the sexy little number I'm wearing is all for you ;)

I smiled and shook my head. She was such a tease.

As long as you know that I'll be ripping said number off that body later tonight.

Her reply beeped through almost instantaneously.

I wouldn't have it any other way.

I groaned and went to get ready. Being in the same room as her was hell. I had to monitor my glances and ensure my attention wasn't completely soaked up by her. It would be so easy for anyone to see there was something between us. At times, I was honestly shocked that nobody had picked up on our relationship.

I checked my reflection in the mirror as I walked out of the bathroom. In my black cargoes, combined with a shirt and my leather jacket, I looked pretty good. I slapped on some aftershave and tousled my hair. There: done. Knowing I was seeing her made me want to put effort into my appearance. Seeing her and not being able to touch and kiss her drove me insane. I wanted her to feel that; I wanted her to feel as crazy as I felt.

Wrenn was the last person I expected to open the door. My mouth dropped. That oh-so-short black dress she was wearing was almost criminal. She looked fucking amazing. Her creamy white legs seemingly went on forever, lengthened by a pair of impossibly high stilettos. She grinned at me, wrapping a strand of hair around her finger as she waited for me to react. *React was right.* She wasn't playing fair.

How the hell was I going to get through tonight with her in the room? How could I not stare at her the entire time? What red-blooded man wouldn't be eyeing her and thinking of all the dirty things he'd like to do to her?

"Hey," I finally said, finding my voice.

"Hi. Come in." She leaned against the wall as I eased past her, moving at a deliberately slow pace, making the most of our contact. She breathed heavily, which made me smile. *I can play that game as well as you.*

"Everyone is through there," she said, pointing to the living room.

I nodded, my eyes leveling on hers. I didn't give a fuck where everyone was. Only her.

"You look fucking amazing," I whispered. I so badly wanted

to kiss her. I wanted to push her back up against that wall and explore her body.

A knock on the door made me jump.

I shook my head, wondering to myself how I'd gotten into this situation. Wrenn went for the door and I went into the living room. It was raining out, so the usual patio gathering had been moved into the inside. Layna waved at me from over near the sofa. I smiled and nodded, saying hello to several colleagues who had also welcomed me.

Throughout dinner, I couldn't keep my eyes off Wrenn.

God knows I tried, but she kept popping up. Her, in that dress—what hope did I have? I was sure everyone I spoke to thought I was an idiot. I'd be deep in conversation, only to drift off mid-thought as she passed me.

"Hey man."

I looked up and saw Mark. "Hey. Didn't even realize you were here," I said with a shake of my head.

"Yeah. You looked like you had a few things on your mind," he said pointedly, jerking his head toward Wrenn. I flushed. *Fuck. If he's noticed, who else has?* He laughed. "It's okay, dude. You're allowed to look. I do it all the time," he added, chuckling, as he turned to check out Wrenn's ass.

I wanted to punch him. I wanted to grab hold of his face and wipe that little smirk off it. I wanted to drag him outside and pulverize him for even *looking* at her. Fists clenched by my sides, I swallowed my anger, willing myself not to react. This possessiveness I felt was so new to me. I excused myself to the bathroom, needing to get away; I needed to pull myself together.

Out of the living room and into the hallway, I leaned against the wall, trying to pull myself together. *This is crazy*. I was going to crack and ruin everything. I was better off faking a headache and leaving. But of course the fact that I'd had a headache would get back to mom…

Wrenn appeared from nowhere, grabbing my hand and leading me away. She took me upstairs, into a room—*her room*—shutting the door behind her.

"You look so *angry*, Mr. Reid," she said, her voice sultry as she wrapped her arms around my waist. She gazed up into my eyes. She was still a few inches shorter than me, even in those heels.

"I can't stand other men even looking at you, Wrenn," I growled.

Her lips found mine as we kissed, and I literally felt my anger melt away. I cupped her face with one hand, my other exploring her bare thigh. She lifted her leg, wrapping it around my waist.

Hoisting her onto my hips, I pushed her back against the wall, desperate for more of her, anything she would give me. I was hard as fuck, and she giggled as her hand brushed past my erection, her eyes smiling up at me.

"I take it you like my dress?" she breathed, her mouth on mine.

"I'd prefer it off you," I growled, my hand at the base of her head, raking through her long, dark hair. We kissed again, my hands running all over her curves. She gasped as I carried her over to her bed and threw her down.

"I don't have a lock on my door," she whispered, her eyes wide.

"What are the chances someone is going to walk in on us?" I asked her, nuzzling her neck. She breathed in deeply as my fingers traced her inner thigh. My tongue began to circle her neck as I ran my index finger along her panties. I felt her legs clench against my hips as she let out a soft moan. "God, I want to taste you," I muttered.

I reached under her dress and pulled her panties down, over her legs, tossing them aside. I pushed her knees apart, chuckling at her mortified expression.

"Has anybody ever gone down on you before?" I asked,

kissing her thigh.

She shook her head violently, making me laugh again.

"Just relax."

I slowly kissed my way down her inner thigh, amazed at how soft her skin was. With each kiss she jumped, knowing that each kiss brought me closer to her sex. I breathed in her scent, running my tongue along the length of her pubic hair. She gasped, her back arching against the sensation of my tongue. Her legs curled around my shoulders, her hand raking through my hair.

God, she tastes good.

My mouth on her, I began to lick, the sensation of my tongue dipping into the softness of her pussy so fucking hot. I could stay here and do this to her all fucking night.

She spread her knees further apart, her hand gripping the back of my hair as my tongue caressed her wetness. She lifted her legs until they rested on my shoulders. Whimpering softly, her fingers traveled up her stomach until they reached her breasts, rolling her nipples between her fingertips, arching her back.

"Oh!" she cried as her hips bucked into me, begging me to go deeper and further inside of her. Curling my arms around her hips, I thrust her toward me as my tongue slammed deep inside her, penetrating her.

"Oh hell yes," she cried, throwing her arm over her mouth to muffle her screams as she began to climax. "God, don't stop," she gasped, again gripping the back of my head. My movements slowed right down. I licked her slowly, enjoying watching her try to squirm out of my grasp. She sat up, her cheeks flushed, pulling me up toward her.

"Holy shit, that was *so* good," she whispered, wrapping her arms around me. Her mouth crushed against mine, her taste still so fresh.

"Wrenn?"

We both froze, staring at each other.

"Just a minute," she called out. "The balcony!" she hissed, her eyes wide with fear.

I nodded and sprung into action. Opening the door just wide enough for me to squeeze out, I disappeared into the darkness. I waited there, catching my breath, my eyes closed as I listened.

"Hey, honey. Have you seen Dalton? He was looking a little off before, and now I can't find him." Layna. I *knew* she was checking up on me. Damn Mom.

"I think I saw him head out the front before? He was on the phone . . ."

"Okay. I better get back downstairs. Are you okay? You're looking a little flushed. Do you have a fever?"

I clamped my hand over my mouth to smother my snigger as Wrenn insisted she was fine. After the door closed I rapped on the balcony door and waited until Wrenn appeared.

"I couldn't go without kissing you again," I said, running my fingers through her hair.

She smiled, her lips meeting mine, the smell of her pussy all around me. "Go," she ordered.

I nodded and walked over to the edge of the balcony where it met the brick exterior of the house. Hoisting myself over the ledge, I let myself drop onto the ground. I stood up and brushed myself off, then walked back inside as if nothing had happened.

Chapter Twenty-Four

Wrenn

A blush crept over my face as I thought about last night.

Dalton, going down on me . . . God, the way I felt when his tongue explored me. That was the most intimate I'd ever been with anyone. Much more intimate than sex, or giving head. As a woman, there was something so personal about having someone go down on you . . . ugh, I couldn't even put it into words.

I stayed in bed for as long as I could, reliving last night. With every thought, my core tingled, aching to feel his touch again. My fingers brushed over my nipples, which stood hard and erect.

Closing my eyes, I thought about him and how good he made me feel. The way his tongue had massaged my clit had me almost coming on the spot. My fingers trailed down between my legs. I imagined him there, kissing, caressing. I slipped a finger inside myself. I was so wet. Thinking about him got me so aroused.

I began to rub harder as the urge to be satisfied began to build. I imagined his erection pressing at my entrance, teasing me.

I thought about the other night, after the hot tub. I'd wanted him so badly that my body ached for him. I circled my clit, reliving the thought of him driving himself inside me and pushing me to the brink. I gasped as my body spasmed, my own touch almost too much to handle.

I softly rubbed my wetness, the euphoria engulfing me until I could take no more. I sighed and rolled over, exhausted and yet so content.

***

I made my way downstairs, thinking about Dalton. God, even the thought of him had me smiling. We were so close to the end, I felt like nothing could ruin this for us.

Except maybe Paige.

Since she'd accosted me the other day, she had stayed out of my way. No more mention of what she thought she knew. She had even stopped her abuse of me.

Dalton was convinced she wouldn't say anything. With no proof, it was our word against hers, and Paige was all about appearances. The last thing she would want to do is snitch. I wished I shared his confidence, but part of me was just waiting for her to do or say something. I knew her well enough to know she wouldn't just back away quietly. That wasn't her style.

As I rounded the corner, I heard Dalton's name. I stopped short, pushing myself up against the wall so Layna wouldn't see me. I strained to hear what she was saying. My heart began to pound. *This was it: Paige had told her. It was over.* I felt dizzy as I struggled to breathe. Oh, God, not like this.

"Honey, I promised you I'd look out for him, and I have been." Layna's voice was soft. Now I was confused. *Honey?* Who was she talking to? Layna chuckled. "You're supposed to worry about him, you're his mother."

I froze. Dalton's mother. This wasn't about us. Relief rushed through me. *Thank fucking God.*

"I know, I understand. I would be, too. What age did Derek start showing symptoms?" Silence. "Uh-huh." More silence.

Who the hell was Derek? And what did they mean 'symptoms?' Of what?

"You're worrying about something that might never happen. If Dalton does turn out to have this disease, you'll deal with it, and you won't be alone. You'll have Dan and me. I have no idea if it's better for him to have the test or not. It's his personal choice whether he wants to know or not."

My heart raced as I tried to process what I was hearing. He might be sick. Dalton might be sick. My brain ached as I ran through all the possible worst-case scenarios in my head. Why hadn't he told me? What was wrong with him?

Oh God, I couldn't handle this.

My legs buckled under me. I lost my balance, crashing into an oversized, poorly positioned vase. My toe throbbed as I hopped around.

"Mary, I have to go." I heard the phone click, and then Layna appeared around the corner. She grabbed my arm to steady me, and helped me over to the sofa.

"Wrenn, what are you doing?" she exclaimed, furrowing her brows.

I shook my head, not sure of what to say. "I was walking down and I heard you on the phone. It sounded like something I shouldn't interrupt, so I waited . . . "

"You eavesdropped?" she clarified, shaking her head in annoyance.

I blushed, not used to being chastised by Layna.

"Honestly Wrenn, that was a private conversation."

"Then maybe you shouldn't have been having it in the middle

of the living room?" I shot back.

She narrowed her eyes and frowned at me.

"So, Dal—Mr. Reid is sick?" I asked, trying to keep the emotion from my voice. Inside, I was a wreck.

Layna sighed and sat down next to me. "He might be. He might be fine. We don't know."

"What 'might be' wrong with him? Is it serious?" I asked. At this point I couldn't care less if my concern sounded misplaced. My heart was racing, a million thoughts flying through my head about what could be wrong with him.

Layna nodded, and then sighed loudly. "I can't talk to you about this, Wrenn. I'm sorry. Try not to worry."

Try not to worry? I was past worrying. In my head, I was already planning his freaking funeral. I jumped up. *I have to get out of here.* If I stayed any longer, everything would come tumbling out. Heading for the door, I grabbed my bag and my keys.

"I'm going to see Kass. I'll speak to you later." I forced myself to sound natural and even managed a smile.

"All right. And Wrenn? Keep this to yourself, okay?"

***

I pulled up outside the river, my hands shaking. It was raining, but I opened my door and stepped out anyway. I needed to feel something, anything, to distract me from the thoughts racing through my head at a million miles an hour. The rain fell down on me, huge, cold drops of water splashing against my face, but I barely noticed. I was soaking wet and I didn't care. The cold air hit me, barely even registering.

He can't be sick. I can't lose him too.

I walked over to the river's edge, kicking at the rocks that lined the path. I dropped down to my knees, sitting in the cold, wet mud as the rain continued to fall around me.

It wasn't fucking fair. Hadn't I been through enough already? Was my life some kind of joke? If there was a God, he was probably up there laughing at poor Wrenn and all her tragedies. It was one thing after another, and I wasn't sure how much more I could handle. I tried so hard to keep myself together and to not dwell on the past, but you've got to be fucking kidding me. This was too much.

And then it hit me, what a horrible person I was.

I'd made all this about me. I couldn't even imagine maybe having some disease that might take hold of me at any moment. Poor Dalton. And his mom. How awful it must be for her, losing her husband and then wondering if the same disease was going to rob her of her son.

For the next hour I sat alone on the bank of the river, sopping wet and freezing cold. My mood changed from feeling sorry for myself to feeling sorry for Dalton, and back again. In the distance, thunder rang through the sky and lightning flashed. I sat there, oblivious. I didn't care about anything.

Except for him.

Chapter Twenty-Five

Dalton

From the comfort of my sofa, I listened to the sound of the storm coming. With the heater on high and my laptop on my knee, I was glad to be inside. The only thing missing was Wrenn—beautiful, sweet Wrenn.

I closed my eyes and imagined her face. Those piercing eyes could stare right into my soul. Her lips, with one kiss, could make all my problems seem pointless and comical. She was perfect. And she was mine.

Next year we could truly be together. Our relationship could be real, and not hidden behind lies and secrets. When I thought about Wrenn, I saw my future as bright, and full of possibilities.

But there was one thing in my way. I needed to tell her. Since I'd kept it from her this entire time, there was no way to do this now without looking like a dick. The thing was, she had made me realize that even if the test came back positive, my life was far from over. This didn't *have* to be the death sentence I saw it as. It could be a blessing. Everyone has to die sometime. I'd have probably ten, maybe twenty years before my symptoms would begin to show, and then probably another ten more.

What scared me the most was living those years without her. She made everything worthwhile. But she had been through so much already. Was it fair of me to expect her to stand by my side and watch me slip away?

My phone buzzed. I dug it out of my pocket and checked the message. It was Wrenn.

I need to talk to you. Can you meet me at the river?

I glanced outside. The rain pounded down heavily against the windowpane. What the hell was she doing out in this weather?

Give me ten minutes.

I could see her in the distance, sitting on the edge of the riverbank, staring out into the storm. *What the fuck was she doing?* I jumped out of the car, the force of the wind hitting me in the face.

"Wrenn!" I yelled.

She tensed, but didn't turn.

I ran over and touched her shoulder, not caring that now I, too, was soaked. "What are you doing out here? Come, get in the car."

She turned to face me, her eyes puffy. She'd been crying. "What's wrong with you?" she asked, her voice overpowering the sound of the rain falling. Her fists were balled up at her sides as she waited for me to say something.

I froze. What did she know?

"What do you mean?" I sputtered, wiping the stream of raindrops off my forehead.

"I heard Layna on the phone with your mom. What the hell is wrong with you, Dalton?"

Oh God, no.

"Come on, Wrenn. Get in the car, and I'll tell you whatever you want to know."

She yanked her hand away from me and stood up. "Just tell me!" she screamed. She was soaked, her white blouse now sheer and clinging to her like a second skin. She shivered as rainwater slowly drizzled down her cheeks. I knew the only way to get her out of this storm was to tell her. With the mood she was in, there was no reasoning with her, not right now.

"My father had a genetic illness called Huntington's disease. There is a fifty percent chance I have it," I said.

She looked up, her eyes dark and full of sadness. Her brows

creased together as she continued to scowl at me. She was angry. Not that I blamed her; I'd be angry with me, too.

"Your father, he died from this?" she demanded.

"Wrenn—"

"Answer the fucking question, Dalton!"

"Yes, okay? Is that what you want to hear? Yes, Wrenn, there is a fifty-fifty chance I might have this wonderful disease that will eventually kill me."

"Were you ever going to tell me?" She wiped her eyes.

I wanted so badly to reach out and comfort her. I nodded.

"When? Because if you were waiting until I'd already fallen for you, you're right on time." She pushed past me and ran to her car.

"Wrenn, will you please talk to me?" I yelled after her.

She didn't stop. I stood there, helpless, as she jumped into her car and took off.

Fuck! I kicked a stray stone into the lake. Of all the scenarios I'd run through in my head of the time I finally told her, this was a thousand times worse.

All I wanted was to spare her pain, but in the process I'd hurt her more. I had lied to her, plain and simple. As soon as we began to get serious, I should've told her. But I hadn't and it became harder and harder as time moved on.

Chapter Twenty-Six

Wrenn

I threw myself down on my bed, not bothering to strip the wet clothes from my body. This couldn't be happening. How could life be so unfair? The thought of losing him was too much. I couldn't go through life with him just waiting for this disease to attack.

I sat up and walked over to my desk. Sitting down, I flicked open my laptop. I typed "Huntington's disease" into Google and clicked on the first link: an entry from the Huntington's Society of America. I'd never even heard of it. I had no idea what it entailed, or what kind of life he could expect if he did in fact have the disease. Would he just drop dead one day? Would there be symptoms? All these questions were racing through my mind, unanswered.

. . . Huntington's disease is a neurodegenerative disease that causes breakdown of brain cells . . .

. . . symptoms include muscle coordination loss, memory loss

and loss of cognitive function . . .

. . . no known cure . . .

. . . life expectancy after initial showing of symptoms is usually ten to twenty years . . .

I slammed the laptop shut and stood up. I felt sick. Reading any more was going to make me feel worse. As amazing as the internet was, when it came to finding correct information, searching while an emotional mess was *not* a good idea.

Grabbing my phone, I deleted the numerous missed calls and texts from Dalton, and called Kass.

"What's up?" Kass answered almost immediately, sounding like her usual upbeat self.

"It's me. I need to get out of here. Will you come with me?" My tone must have told her this was serious, because for once she didn't question me.

"Of course. I'll be there in ten."

Hanging up, I shoved a change of clothes into an overnight bag along with my brush and toothbrush. Zipping it up, I went downstairs. Thank God everyone was out. I left Layna a note saying I'd gone out with Kass and would be back the next day. Before I went outside, I fished around in the bottom drawer for the spare key to the beach house. My fingers finally grasped hold of it. Shoving it into my pocket, I went outside to wait for Kass.

***

True to her word, ten minutes later Kass pulled into the driveway. I climbed into the passenger seat and clicked on my seatbelt. Kass glanced at me with concern as she backed out of the driveway.

"Are you okay?"

"Not really." I muttered. I put my head back and closed my eyes. "Can we go to Cinter Beach? My aunt has a holiday house there."

Kass nodded. For the first time ever, she was speechless. She could see I was upset, and I think she didn't know whether to try and get me to talk or not.

The first fifteen minutes of our drive were spent in total silence. Kass was focused on driving, and me, I was lost in my thoughts. Sighing, I stared out the window. The storm had passed, but the day was still miserable, reflecting my mood perfectly.

"He might be sick."

Kass whipped her head around, alarmed. Her brown eyes were full of concern as she waited for me to continue.

"Dalton," I clarified. "He might be dying."

"What do you mean?" Kass said carefully. Her hands clenched the steering wheel as she glanced intermittently at me.

I snorted. "I don't know. He might have a genetic disease that is terminal, but it won't show up for years. Decades, even. But it will, eventually, kill him."

"Oh, Wrenn. Shit, that's bad. There is no way to find out whether he has it?" she asked softly.

I shrugged. What did I know? Nothing.

She reached over to me, her hand closing over mine. "I'm so sorry, Wrenn."

"He didn't even tell me himself, Kass. I overhead Layna on the phone to his mom. How could he not tell me something like that?"

I shook my head, still so angry. I deserved to know if the guy I was falling in love with was going to die. I deserved to fucking know, dammit. I felt cheated. Betrayed. Would knowing that have changed the way I'd felt about him? It didn't change who he was, but it might have affected my decision to chase him.

"Maybe he didn't know how to broach it. I can't imagine it would be an easy conversation to start," she reasoned.

I glanced at her.

Maybe she was right. I gazed out the window again, closing my eyes. Maybe he was trying to protect me. I could've gone the next twenty years not knowing that I might lose him. Would that have been better than this?

I didn't know. God, I was so confused.

***

"Wrenn."

I opened my eyes and glanced around. Cinter Beach. Where I had spent the majority of my childhood vacations. Smooth, white sand that stretched for miles, crystal clear water, cute little ice cream stores that stayed open late into the night. Not so much in the dead of winter, though.

I had so many memories. Remembering made me sad. It made me wish Mom was there so I could talk to her. What advice would she give me? Forgetting for a moment that Dalton was my teacher, Mom would've told me to go with my heart. True, unconditional love was such a rare thing to find that a short time was better than not experiencing it at all.

"Up on the hill. The one with the white fence," I mumbled, realizing that Kass was waiting for directions. As she drove along the boulevard, memories of my childhood came rushing back: Dad, teaching me how to body board; eating ice cream on the beach with Mom and Layna; fighting with Jordan over which room was mine. I wiped a stray tear from my eye.

Kass pulled into the driveway. I opened the door and stepped out. We walked up the steps together to the front door. I hadn't been there since the summer before the accident. As I walked to the door, a sense of peace overwhelmed me, despite the crazy memories flooding back. I felt close to my family here, close like I hadn't felt in weeks—months, even.

Inside, we walked through to the kitchen. Everything looked just as it had two years ago, but for a thin layer of dust covering the sofa and the small glass coffee table lying in front of it. I walked out the back, over to the fuse box, and clicked on the power and water. Inside, the kitchen lit up and the fridge came to life.

"This place is nice," muttered Kass, turning full circle, her expression one of awe. "You've been hiding this little gem from me," she accused.

"I'd forgotten about it," I admitted, sinking into an oversized leather armchair.

Kass joined me, sinking into its twin. Maybe 'forgotten' was the wrong word. I'd pushed this place out of my mind so I didn't have to deal with the memories.

"Do you wanna talk about it?" Kass asked gently.

"I don't know what there is to say." Would talking change anything? Nope. "Do you know anything about Huntington's disease?" I half joked.

She shook her head. "And please tell me you haven't Googled it," she added.

I winced.

"Wrenn! God, stay off the freaking computer. Talk to Dalton. You have questions, ask him. God," she said again, shaking her head. "Didn't you learn that time you thought you had cancer because Dr. Google analyzed your symptoms?"

Obviously not.

I checked my phone. Twenty missed calls. I held it up so Kass could see. She groaned and shook her head. I knew what she was thinking: give the poor guy a break. Only, I wasn't ready to. I didn't trust myself to get through a sentence without bursting into tears. I needed time to digest all of this. I needed time to figure out what my next move was.

"I'm going for a walk," I mumbled, standing up.

"Do you want me to come?" Kass asked.

I shook my head. I needed some space. I needed time alone to figure out my head. I leaned over and hugged her, knowing how lucky I was to have a friend like her.

***

About a five minute walk down the road and off a dirt track was the little swimming spot where we used to go. The white sandy stretch of beach was sheltered by huge oak trees which made it the perfect spot to relax.

I walked over and sat down on the broken tree that served as a seat. I ran my fingers over the engravings carved into the wood, one in particular catching my eye: *Best summer ever, 2009.*

I had been fourteen that summer. We had come down to the beach house for the entire summer vacation, and I had met a boy. It was that summer I had my first kiss. I smiled as I remembered telling Mom after it had happened. We'd sat up late drinking hot cocoa, talking about things, and somehow the conversation became about him.

I couldn't even remember the boy's name. Sam or Steve or something. I never saw or heard from him again, but it was the closeness I felt to Mom that I'd cherish forever.

Kicking off my shoes, I walked over to the edge of the shore and dipped my toes in the freezing water. I watched as the tiny waves lapped at my feet before being soaked up into the sand, then falling back into the sea.

My mind turned to Dalton. I thought about how special he made me feel. Nobody had made me feel that way in such a long time. It sucked this was happening, but it didn't change the way I felt about him.

It didn't change the fact that I was in love with him.

Chapter Twenty-Seven

Dalton

I paced the bedroom with my hands on my head, waiting for her to call. Or text. Anything. God, I was such an idiot. Her finding this out was bad enough, but to not hear it from me? That was worse. So much worse.

"Fuck!" I kicked the wall, instantly regretting it as a large hole appeared, about the size of my shoe. I watched as little fragments of plaster fell away to the floor. See, this was why I'd avoided relationships. How could you plan your future when you might not have one?

We found out my dad had Huntington's when I was four. The fact that he had it meant one of his parents would have also had it. His being adopted at age one meant the genetic risk was not identified until it was too late.

Dad was forty-two when he was diagnosed with the disease, and fifty-three when he died. His diagnosis was the reason they'd decided not to have any more children. His progression had been fast, much faster than usual, but the speed of progression was also a genetic factor. Did it mean I would develop symptoms earlier and faster? Possibly.

Basically, when it boiled down to it, if I did have the mutation, there was a fifty percent chance that I would display symptoms by the age of forty. A simple little test could potentially tell me with one hundred percent accuracy whether I had the disease or not. But was that something I wanted to know?

Until now, not knowing had been better than finding out I had it. Not knowing gave me hope. But now it wasn't just me; I had to think of Wrenn. If she even still wanted to be with me.

I picked up my phone and dialed Mom, needing her advice. She had been trying to get me to have the test for years, without success. She would want to know why I'd suddenly changed my mind.

"Dalton." She sounded surprised to hear from me.

"Hey, Mom," I said, sitting down on the edge of the bed. I rubbed the back of my neck, trying to relieve some of the tension from the last few days. "How are you?"

"Good. Is something wrong? You sound upset."

"No, everything is fine. I've just been thinking . . . I think I want to get tested." Mom was silent. I waited a moment to let my words sink in before the barrage of questions started.

"What's brought this on?" she asked. "I'm glad you've decided to find out, but you've always been so adamant about not being tested."

"I know, but things have changed. I need to know, one way or the other. I need to live, Mom. I can't keep waiting for something that might not happen. No matter how much I try and push it away, it's always there, eating at me."

"I'll call Dr. Martin and arrange it," Mom said, referencing the doctor who'd cared for Dad while he was alive. Apparently, he was one of the top Huntington's specialists in the country.

"Okay. Thanks, Mom." I felt a sense of relief. I was one step closer to knowing my fate. After I ended the call, I tried Wrenn again. I nearly fainted when Kass answered.

"Dalton." She sounded tired.

"Kassia. Is Wrenn there? Will she speak to me?" I asked, trying to keep the sheer desperation out of my voice.

"Look, we're at her aunt's holiday house. 430 The Boulevard, Cinter Beach. If you come down, I'll disappear for a few hours."

"God, thank you Kassia. I'm on my way."

***

I knocked on the door to the beach house, still unsure of my game plan.

An hour in the car, and I still had nothing. Really, what was there to say? I could apologize all day for not telling her, but I knew deep down that wasn't the real issue.

Kass opened the door. She smiled and let me in. "She's in the living room, down the end and to the right." She slipped out the door, shutting it behind her.

I walked down the hallway of the huge house. Everything was so perfect, so new—it was like a display home. And strangely, it was all so familiar. I felt like I had been there before.

Wrenn was curled up on the sofa, facing away from me. I edged closer, my heart racing. The TV was on low. She turned around, her eyes wide, shocked at the sight of me. I thought I saw a glimmer of a smile, but as quickly as it was there, it was gone. Emotion after emotion swept through her eyes: shock, happiness, sorrow, and then confusion.

"You're here," she said, wiping her eyes. "Let me guess. Kass?"

I nodded, and walked around the sofa.

She sat up, allowing me to sit down next to her. I put my hand on her thigh, over her faded jeans. She wore an old blue sweatshirt, and her hair was tangled and unbrushed, tied up in a pony tail. Regardless, she looked beautiful.

"I'm sorry I didn't tell you earlier," I muttered, taking her hand in mine.

"I did some research." She turned to look at me. "So this test can tell you if you have it, and when you'll show symptoms?" She looked so scared, I just wanted to wrap my arms around her and take away the pain.

"It will tell me if I carry the disease. It can suggest how early I will display symptoms, but it's not accurate regarding the symptoms." I tried to explain, but there was so much to tell. I'd had all my life to learn about this disease, and there was shit that I myself still didn't know.

"How old was your dad?" she asked. "When the symptoms began?"

"Forty-two. Though he was symptomatic for a couple of years beforehand but they couldn't say for sure if that was the Huntington's or not."

"Did they know there was a chance when they had you? That he had it?" she asked.

I shook my head. "Dad was adopted. He never knew his real

parents." I took a deep breath. "Look, Wrenn, I understand if this is too much for you. I get it. That's why I tried to distance myself from you early on. You lost your family. I couldn't imagine putting you through losing me too."

Tears welled in her eyes as she took in what I was saying. "I don't want to *not* be with you, Dalton, but the idea of losing you? I don't know if I can handle that," she said quietly.

I took her hand in mine, entwining our fingers together. "You don't need to decide now. In fact, I don't want you to. I want you to think about it for as long as you need to." I paused, the next sentence sticking in my throat. "I'm having the test," I added quietly.

"You are?" she said, her eyes widening.

"I am. I want to know. Being with you made me realize I need to know the truth." I sighed, so angry at the situation. "Wrenn, I need you to be fully informed. If I do have Huntington's, you deserve to know exactly what it means. Ask me anything."

"Huh?"

'You said you Googled. That means you have questions. Ask me anything and I'll do my best to answer."

She turned her body toward me, unsure and afraid. She didn't say anything for a while, she just sat there, staring at the floor.

"What are the symptoms?" she finally asked quietly.

"The most common symptom usually noticed first is muscle twitching. Involuntary movement, that kind of thing. Other symptoms are restlessness, clumsiness, dropping things, and tripping." I paused, watching her intently. "There can also be mental symptoms such as depression, memory loss, impulsiveness…"

"How does it kill you? I mean, you said your dad died from it," she asked in a small voice.

"The disease itself doesn't kill, it's things like pneumonia, choking on food, and organ failure that cause eventual death."

"Oh," she said, her eyes dropping to the floor. "How quickly does it progress? Was your dad able to walk before he died? I mean, was he mobile?"

I shook my head and cleared my throat. Talking about Dad made the seriousness of this begin to sink in. "No. The last few months, he was in a nursing home. He couldn't walk, talk, or even eat. It progresses slowly, but you can't underestimate how hard those final few years will be, Wrenn. If I have this…you will watch me slowly slip away. I'll need help with everything, from eating to bathing…" My voice trailed off as I struggled to contain my emotions. This was as honest as I'd ever been with myself about the disease, and the thought of her seeing me like that…

Fuck, I'd *kill* myself before putting her through that.

I don't want to think about this right now. I need her. If she can't be with me, then I'll deal with that, but right now I need her.

"Can we forget about this, Wrenn? Just for tonight? I want one night with you where I don't have to worry about hurting you. I know that's a lot to ask, but if I have to let you go, I really need this."

She nodded and squeezed my hand. "Can you take me home tomorrow? I'll tell Kass she can go."

I nodded and leaned over to kiss her, my mouth brushing past her soft lips. I pulled away and stared at her, wanting to memorize every little detail of her face. She brought her hand up to my neck and pulled me to her, our lips connecting again, this time in a slow, intense kiss that took my breath away.

"Will you sleep with me?" she asked, her voice anxious. "I just want your arms holding me. I've never felt as safe as I do when I'm in your embrace."

I nodded and let her lead me upstairs.

We entered a bedroom. A mirror hung on the wall, and a small chest of drawers stood in the corner. We walked over to the large bed under the window. Curving my arms under her thighs and around her back, I lifted her onto the bed, pulling the covers over her. Then I climbed in, wrapping her in my arms. I stroked her arm tenderly. This disease…it had the ability to rob me of the simplest indulgences, like holding the woman I loved close to me. I stroked her arm until she fell asleep, then listened to the sound of her chest rising and falling.

I'd avoided falling in love for this very reason. This fucked up disease had ruined my family. How could I drag someone I loved into that world? At least the test would give me closure. I'd know. One way or the other, I would know for sure, and Wrenn would have all the facts. She deserved to know everything, because this would affect her whole life. Even having kids was an issue…but at least there were tests nowadays and ways to eradicate the disease being passed on. My head rested against hers. I closed my eyes, listening to her breathe.

If these are my final few moments with her, then I want to remember them forever.

***

Rolling over, I wrapped my arm around Wrenn's waist. Only she wasn't there. I sat up in shock, the stark morning sunshine almost blinding me. I pulled my phone out of my pocket.

It was after eleven. How had I slept so late? And where was Wrenn?

I climbed out of bed, adjusting my jeans. Walking out into

the hall, I glanced each way, looking for a sign of Wrenn. Making my way down to the kitchen, I called out her name. No answer.

Why the fuck did this place look so familiar? I was *sure* I'd been here before. I walked outside and down the steps into the backyard. A cobblestone path led through the manicured lawn, around the back of a large garage.

"Wrenn?" I called out.

I heard her voice faintly in the distance. Walking towards it, what looked like a cubby house came into view from behind a cluster of bushes. I breathed in the salty air, something you can only experience near the ocean. I loved it out here.

"Where are you?" I called out.

"In here." Her muffled voice was coming from inside the cubby house. I leaned down and stepped through the doorway. My breath caught in my throat as memories began flooding back.

Wrenn and I.

We had met before. This hideous pink cubby house, that's why this place felt so familiar. Eleven years ago, in this very place, she had made me realize that I needed to live my life. All these years later, we had found our way back to each other.

"What is it?" she asked, alarmed.

I shook my head, not sure what to say, or how to say it. "I've been here before, Wrenn. We've met before. That first day in school I *knew* you. You were so familiar to me, but I just couldn't place you. I assumed it was just from class, but it wasn't. You remember telling me that my mom probably knew your mom? Well, they did! We met at a party. You would've been about seven, and I was twelve."

She shook her head, looking at me like I was crazy, and laughed. Yes, I sounded insane, and that was okay because this was fucking unbelievable. What were the odds? I mean, considering our connection with Layna, it wasn't that farfetched, but for this woman I was in love with to be the same girl who'd changed my outlook all those years ago…I was stunned.

"You don't remember me at all, do you?" I chuckled.

"No, sorry. You obviously left a lasting impression on me," she joked.

I walked over to her and took her hand, kneeling down in front of her. She parted her legs, allowing me between them. I hugged her body, my lips nuzzling the nape of her neck.

"You did exactly that with me," I said softly. "Not in a creepy way. You just spelled it out to me, so innocently, that I was wasting my life waiting to get sick."

Wrenn looked puzzled. "How did I know you were going to get sick?"

"We came out here to get away from our parents. They were talking about me, and Dad's illness. You looked up at me and said, 'So what? We're all going to get sick.'" I smiled, squeezing her hand. "You said something nobody had ever bothered to say. You made me realize that just because I *might* get sick one day, it didn't make me special. Or different."

"Wow," she mumbled, furrowing her brows together. "That's pretty incredible, huh?"

"No," I replied, kissing her lips. "*You're* pretty incredible."

Chapter Twenty-Eight

Dalton

I collapsed into bed late Sunday night, too tired to bother showering, or even undressing. I was exhausted.

I'd barely gotten any sleep the night before. I'd spent most of it lying in bed with Wrenn curled up in my arms, watching her sleep. I loved the way her lip twitched, and how every few minutes she'd sigh. It was like I couldn't let myself fall asleep because I wanted to remember every second with her.

Now we were back on campus, back to reality. It was ironic that being back in the real world meant going back to pretending to be I was something I wasn't. We only had to get through one more week, and then things would be easier. I still didn't know how we were going to break the news to Layna—or even if there was any news to break. Wrenn had a lot of thinking to do, and I didn't want to assume she would decide to be with me just because of last night.

***

The following afternoon, I was sitting in the teacher's lounge when Layna came in. "Dalton, can I see you for a moment. In my office?"

I nodded, eyeing her expression. She wouldn't meet my eyes.

God, she knows. Fuck.

I followed her into her office, all the classic signs of a panic attack beginning to manifest inside me: the shaking hands, the rapid heartbeat, and the pit in my stomach. I took a seat at her desk, trying to hide my shaking hands by positioning them under my thighs.

What was my best move here? Wait for the accusations to begin, or get everything on the table now, first?

"Dalton, there's no easy way to say this . . . " She sighed as she sat down, her hands clenched together on her desk. "There has been an accusation made against you."

"An accusation?" I repeated, shocked. My mind wandered to Wrenn. There was no way in hell . . . would she? I mean, she was confused about us right now, but she would never do that.

"A student has made a claim against you . . . " She stopped and took a breath. "Gosh, I don't even know how to phrase this. Have you had any inappropriate dealings with Paige Warner?"

"Paige?" I almost shouted. Part of me felt relief. The rest of me wondered what the fuck Paige had told her. "Never. I've never even been alone with her, other than a minute or two before or after class. What is she saying I did?"

"Ms. Warner is saying that you asked her to your room last night. She claims that you forced yourself on her."

"She told you that I *raped* her?" I said, incredulous.

What the fuck? Last night I had been with Wrenn, fifty miles from this place. I'd worked myself up so much expecting this to be about Wrenn that my body was in panic mode. It was Paige's word against mine, and the only way to clear my name would be to admit my relationship with Wrenn.

Fuck. Once these things got out, it didn't matter if I was innocent or not, my career would be in the shitter.

"She said that you intimidated her into having sex with you. She is not saying you raped her, but she is saying she felt she couldn't say no, given your position."

"And that's not rape?" I asked sarcastically. "What happens now?"

"I need to notify the school board and let them know. Then I will have to inform the police."

Holy shit.

This was crazy. I had no idea what the fuck was going through that girl's head. Why the hell would she make up such lies? Was this all because I shot down her advances?

"Dalton, if this isn't true, we will get to the bottom of it." Layna looked at me sympathetically.

"Right, because an indecent assault investigation will have no influence on my future employment prospects at all," I growled. I felt bad for snapping at Layna. She was just doing her job. "I'm sorry. I understand that you're in a difficult position."

She smiled at me and nodded. "We will sort this out, Dalton. Try not to worry. In the meantime, I'm going to have to suspend you. It might be an idea for you to stay off campus for a few days while the police complete their investigation."

I nodded curtly, and stood up. "If that's all, I will go and collect some of my things."

***

"She what?" Wrenn squeaked. Her reaction was the same as mine: horrified and angry. "What the . . . I mean, you were with me . . . oh, that *bitch*."

"What?" I said, balancing the phone on my shoulder as I packed my bag.

"That little slut! I know *exactly* what her game is, Dalton. She doesn't want to rat on us, so the next best thing is to make us expose ourselves."

Holy shit, Wrenn was right.

Paige knew the only way for me to truly clear my name was to admit my affair with Wrenn. She knew I was with Wrenn the night before. How, I don't know, but it all made sense: she was so threatened by Wrenn that she would do anything to destroy her—and me, it seemed.

"I can't believe it," I muttered.

"So what now? You just leave?"

"I can't just leave, I'm under police investigation. The school is putting me up in a hotel for a few nights," I replied glumly.

"Which hotel?" she asked.

"Wrenn, that is such a bad idea . . ."

"I know. But not seeing you will be torture," she muttered.

"Does that mean you forgive me?" I asked, holding my breath.

"I forgive you. I mean, I understand why you didn't tell me, and it doesn't change how I feel about you…" her voice trailed off.

"But?" I prodded gently.

"I need to think. But that doesn't mean I don't want to see you. Even though we can't, anyway."

"We can see each other, just not there. Maybe speak to Kass and see if she has any ideas on where we could meet?"

"Good idea. I'll talk to her today," Wrenn replied. "I better go. Layna just got home. Text me later?"

"Okay. Bye." I hung up, still reeling over what had happened. Though I knew I'd done nothing wrong where Paige was concerned, I couldn't see this ending well.

***

The motel on the edge of town was dark and seedy, and apparently all the school thought I was worth. The stained sheets made the bed look uninviting, and the scratching sound of cockroaches digging around on the floor made my stomach turn. I texted Wrenn to let her know I was okay. There was no point letting her know how bad this place was; I was already worried she was going to come clean to Layna. I didn't need to give her more reason to.

I couldn't stay there. Grabbing my bag, I exited the motel room, slamming the door shut behind me. I'd rather sleep in my car than in that shithole. I threw my bag in the back and slid into the drivers seat. I searched on my phone for a hotel in Hollisbrook. I'd stay one night there and then go to Mom's. If the police wanted to speak to me, they could do so there.

After booking a room and going inside, I threw my bag down on the floor and collapsed onto the bed. How the hell did things get this fucked up? I dreaded what the police were going to ask me. Had I been inappropriate with a student at the school? *Well technically, yes, but it's not what you think!* Yeah right, that was going to go down well.

***

What the hell was that?

It was pitch black. It took me a moment to remember where I was and why I was there. I fumbled blindly for a bedside lamp. My fingers grasped the cord. Light filled the room.

Bang, bang, bang.

I jumped up and headed for the door. Wrenn stood there, frowning at me. She ducked inside and shut the door.

"You look like shit," she observed.

"Thanks." I rubbed my aching head. "How did you know I was here?" I croaked.

She gave me a strange look. "You messaged me." She leaned

over, and for a second I thought she was going to kiss me. "Have you been drinking?"

Had I? I glanced over at the minibar, and the several empty bottles that lay scattered over the counter. Well, that explained a few things.

She walked over to them and disposed of the empty bottles in the garbage. Next, she took the coffee pot and half-filled it with water, then coffee, before plugging it in. In the back of my mind stuck the words 'memory loss.' Like every other time any possible symptom surfaced, the question raced through my mind: was this the beginning? Did I have it?

Even a few weeks ago, the phone slipping out of my grasp at Wrenn's. I'd gotten out of there so fast after that.

"I'm going to tell Layna everything," Wrenn announced.

"Wrenn, don't—"

"Do you have a better idea?" she asked, spinning around, her eyebrows raised.

I shut my mouth. *No, I didn't.* I sank onto the bed and sighed. Wrenn sat next to me and reached for my hand. She was so warm. How did she do that?

"Look, she'll be angry, but whatever she does it has to be

better than the alternative, right? As soon as the police start questioning you, our secret is going to come out." The coffee maker boiled. She stood up and filled two cups with coffee and cream.

"Thanks," I muttered, taking the coffee from her outstretched hand. "I'm going to stay at Mom's for a few days. I can't stay here, staring at there walls. It's driving me crazy.

"So I won't see you?"

"I'll give it a few days and see where this goes. Hopefully I'll be back before you even start missing me," I said. I set the coffee down and reached for her hand, pulling her onto my lap.

She sat, straddling me, my arms around her waist. Even a few days away from her was too long, but I couldn't stay where I was.

"I already miss you," she mumbled, frowning.

I kissed the tip of her nose and rested my forehead against hers.

"I can barely get through a few hours without you, Dalton." Her voice cracked as she closed her eyes, refusing to look at me.

Gently I lifted her chin, my lips pressing against hers. As we kissed, arousal began to build inside me. I slipped my hand under her sweater, running my fingers along the curve of her spine. She sighed as my lips found her neck.

Her fingers closing around the hem of her sweater, she lifted it over her head. God, she was so fucking sexy. I kissed hers breasts around the cup of her lacy black bra, pulling it down to expose her soft skin. My mouth fondled her nipple until it sat erect.

"I want you so fucking bad, Wrenn."

She kissed me and then stood up, wiggling out of her jeans. Pushing me back on the bed, she reached for my belt, unbuckling both it and my pants. I lifted my hips, letting her pull them down, along with my boxers, until they pooled in a pile on the floor. My cock ached for her as she kneeled down. Taking the tip in her mouth, she began to suck.

Oh lord. Fuck yes. Her tongue ran along the length of me as her soft lips worked my cock. My hands found her head, my fingers raking through her long, silky hair. There was something incredibly erotic about watching her as she sucked, her eyes firmly on me, like she knew the power she had over me.

"Come here," I panted, reaching for my wallet. I pulled out a condom and rolled it over my erection. Taking her hand, I helped her onto the bed, lowering her onto my length. She groaned as I slid inside her, grinding against me as I rocked her back and forth.

My fingers roamed up her bare waist, running over her

breasts, squeezing them in my hands, then back down, clutching onto her hips, thrusting myself deeper inside of her.

"Oh God, yes," she gasped. She bent over me, her breasts spilling in my face as she rode my length. I curled my tongue around her nipple and sucked hard, making her scream out. "I'm going to come. Oh God, yes!" she cried as I rocked her faster.

Oh God, what this woman did to me.

I gasped as I released, her nails digging into the skin on my chest, the pain nonexistent in the midst of the orgasm I was experiencing. She drove me crazy and pressed every single button, sending everything about me into overdrive.

She collapsed beside me on the bed, panting heavily. I rolled over and spooned her, exhausted and content. I knew she couldn't stay, but even a few minutes with her in my arms was worth everything.

Chapter Twenty-Nine

Wrenn

Even before I left Dalton, I'd made up my mind to tell Layna everything. I couldn't see the point in keeping us a secret any longer. There was no other way out of this mess for Dalton, and in a week none of it would matter. The only problem was Dalton's career—but Paige had pretty much made sure that was a bust.

Dan was out when I got home. I was glad. This was going to be hard enough with just Layna. She would tell Dan, and I was fine with that, but telling both of them together was way too overwhelming. I found Layna in her office, eyebrows creased and deep in thought, poring over papers. I rapped on the door. She looked up and smiled.

"Can I talk to you about something?" I asked her, walking over and sitting down opposite her, my hands clasped tightly together in my lap.

"You can always talk to me. What's up?" she asked, taking

her glasses off.

I held my hands together to try and combat the uncontrollable shaking in them. I was honestly terrified of what she was going to say. "I need to tell you something. I know you're going to be angry, but I hope you can at least listen to what I'm telling you and be open-minded."

Layna frowned at me. "You're scaring me, Wrenn. Are you pregnant?" she gasped.

I snorted and shook my head. God, no—though maybe her thinking that was a good thing? Maybe that lessened the impact of what I had to tell her? *I wish.*

"I've been seeing someone." I swallowed hard, the huge lump in my throat not moving. "He is the most amazing guy I've ever met. Around him I feel special. Like I'm one in a million. He makes me want more for myself. He makes me want to live, not just exist. I honestly can't explain how deep my feelings for him are, Layna. There just aren't words to do it justice."

"Well, that's good," Layna said nervously, smoothing her blonde hair with her hands. "When are you getting to the part I'll hate?"

"It's coming," I assured her with a grin. "You're not going to be happy when you hear who this guy is." I paused for a moment, rubbing my lips together. "Dalton."

"Dalton?" gasped Layna, her mouth dropping open. "As in…"

"Yes."

"Oh, Wrenn. Why? How? Did you instigate this or did he?" Layna's eyes welled up with tears, her hand flying to her mouth.

"It wasn't like that, Layna. It just happened. Please don't be angry at him. If anything, I pushed for us to be together." I was trying so hard to explain, but no matter what I said, he was always going to be my teacher who took advantage of me.

"Come on, Wrenn. He's your teacher, of course he's at fault. He abused his position of power. Regardless of how it might feel, he took advantage of you." She was past being upset and had moved straight into anger. Anger that was directed at him.

"But I'm eighteen," I argued. "I'm an adult. There is no law stopping us from being together—"

"Again, that doesn't matter! This school prides itself on its reputation. How do you think this will look to our investors? And I can tell you right now this does nothing to help his case against Paige." She stood up, pacing the small space in her office, every now and then stopping to shake her head.

"That's why I'm telling you this. I know he wasn't with Paige that night, because he and I were at the vacation house in Cinter Beach. Paige is *lying*." I sighed and shook my head.

This was such a mess. I felt like all I had done was make things worse. Fuck Paige. This was all her fault. If she had kept her filthy lying mouth shut, none of this would be happening. Of course, that didn't change the fact that Layna would've found out eventually. She wasn't stupid; she would've put it together and realized what we'd been doing.

"She made a pass at him, he shot her down, she wanted revenge. She knew about him and me, and she knew that I would do anything to protect him, even if it meant ruining my relationship with you," I explained softly.

Layna was quiet for a moment. "You could never ruin our relationship," she said, wrapping her arms around me. "I'm shocked, Wrenn, and disappointed. This is a lot to take in. But no matter what, Dan and I will always love you and be here for you." She sat down next to me, taking my hand in hers. "This is why you were so upset after hearing me on the phone with his mother." Her eyes welled up again. "God, I'm so sorry you had to find out that way."

"So you've known all along that Dalton might have this…disease?" I finished.

Layna nodded, her eyes full of sadness. "I take it he's told you what it is?"

I nodded.

"His father was a wonderful man. It was so hard for his mother to watch him suffer like that. Are you sure you're ready for that, Wrenn?"

"No," I admitted, "but I'm not ready to let him go, either. So what choice do I have? I'm thinking about it. Everything. I haven't given him an answer yet."

Layna nodded. "You're a very mature young woman. Most girls your age wouldn't be thinking so far into the future, but you have your life pretty much planned out. I admire that."

I smiled, her words meaning more to me than I could express. I was so sure she wouldn't understand, and she'd been more supportive than I ever could've imagined.

"I'm not even sure what I'm doing," I admitted honestly.

"No, but the fact that you're thinking so deeply about things says a lot."

I moved forward, fiddling with my fingernails as I worked up the courage to ask her what was on my mind—things I had been too afraid to ask Dalton, morbid things that I couldn't get out of my head. Every time I thought to myself that I couldn't do it, I'd think about not being with him and realize that leaving him wasn't an option. I *had* to do it. More than that, I had to suck it up and stop being such a selfish child. This wasn't about me. Not really. The picture was so much bigger than what I was feeling at the moment.

"Layna? Dalton's dad—did you know him well? I don't know much about this disease, only what I found on Google and what Dalton has told me."

"Yes, I knew him well. He was a proud man who didn't like to be fussed over. That made the whole thing so much worse." She sighed and shook her head sadly, her eyes clouding over with memories.

"How do you mean?" I asked, my voice small.

"The disease robbed him of all his independence, Wrenn. Even the smallest thing, he needed assistance with. Early on in his diagnosis it wasn't so bad, but as things progressed…it was hard, even for me, a person outside of their circle, to watch." She looked at me earnestly. "I'm not going to lie to you, Wrenn. How Mary and Dalton coped with that is beyond me. Huntington's disease is relentless. It's a terrible, horrible illness. And it's not just the physical symptoms you need to watch out for. Things like depression and other mental illnesses are common symptoms that can occur way before any physical symptoms kick in."

"What scares me the most is losing him. I don't know if I can handle that. How can I be strong for him when I can't cope with things myself?" My voice broke.

Layna stood me up and hugged me again, her warm embrace comforting. "You're stronger than you think, honey. And there is so much love and passion inside of you. Your mom would be very proud, you know that?"

I nodded, wiping my eyes. She would be proud of me. Not so much the falling for the teacher thing, but everything else. How I'd handled everything I'd been through the past year. And now this.

"God, Wrenn, I can't be mad at you. Everything should horrify me, both as *your* aunt and as *his* boss, but both of you have been through so much. And no matter what, you'll always have me. Whatever you decide, and whenever you need me, I'll be right by your side. You won't be in this alone, honey."

"Thanks," I mumbled. "That means a lot to hear you say that."

I rubbed the side of my head and stifled a yawn, only just realizing how tired I was. The last couple of days had been huge, and so stressful I'd only managed a few hours of sleep.

"So what happens now? Is this enough to get Paige's claim thrown out?" I asked nervously.

"It will certainly be enough to create doubt in her story. And if you're right and all she wants is to ruin you, then your admittance should be enough for her to drop her accusation."

"And Dalton? How will this affect his career?"

Layna shook her head. "Unfortunately, that's not completely up to me. I'll do my best for this not to go on his record, but I can't promise you anything. You should stay away from him for a few days, though, Wrenn. It will be best for both him and you. Until this is cleared up. Until after your graduation."

I nodded and hugged her again, wondering how I was going to go without seeing him, but at the same time relieved I had the time I needed to think. Without the distraction of him.

Chapter Thirty

Wrenn

The eve of my graduation. One more day until I was free.

One more day until I could start the rest of my life, and I still hadn't worked out what to do. I refused to commit to Dalton unless I was sure.

God, that sounded horrible. As bad as this felt for me, it had to be worse for him. He didn't need me changing my mind in five years, or ten years. If I was with him, it was for all of it.

I tried to put things into perspective—life with Dalton, and life without him. My feelings for him were beyond love. I loved this man more than I did anything else in my world right now. If he *did* have this disease, was twenty years with him enough? Was it better than not having him at all? I couldn't imagine loving anybody the way I did him. That had to count for something.

Kass took me shopping for a graduation dress, mostly to take my mind off Dalton and everything else that was going on. Paige had recounted her accusations against Dalton, but the board had insisted on investigating my relationship with him. After countless interviews with various members of the school board, they were meeting today to decide his fate, and I was a nervous wreck.

I hadn't seen or spoken to him all week. We had sent texts—a *lot* of texts—but it wasn't the same as hearing his voice. I longed to hear that deep, husky voice whispering sexy and dirty things into my ear.

"How about this?"

Kass held out a short purple-and-black chiffon dress. I screwed up my nose at the wide straps. I didn't do straps. They made my shoulders look huge. I searched through the rack in front of me, only half focused on the task at hand.

"There, what about that?" she said.

I stopped at looked at the dress I was holding in my hands. Okay, this one wasn't half bad. It was strapless, long, and fitted with a built-in corset. I ran the dark blue silk fabric over my fingers, loving the way it felt against my skin. This was perfect.

The winter formal was set to follow the small, informal ceremony for the half dozen students graduating early. It wasn't usual for students graduating early to have a midyear ceremony, but Layna had insisted on marking the occasion.

"I'll try it on," I agreed, carrying it into the dressing room. I stripped out of my jeans and shirt, and my bra. Lifting the dress carefully over my head, I let it shimmy down over my body and over my hips.

Wow. I stared at my refection in the mirror. This dress was stunning. I pushed open the door and called out for Kass.

"Holy shit, I hope you're getting that dress," she gasped, covering her mouth. "You look fucking amazing. You're making me second guess *my* dress."

I looked back at myself, tilting my head. It was perfect, but it was also expensive. When Layna gave me her credit card for a dress, I was pretty sure she didn't have this budget in mind. Still, I had a lot of savings put away. And I hadn't brought myself anything in a long time...

Okay. I was sold. All I could think was *wait until Dalton sees me in this dress*, even if it was a few days after the dance.

***

After we finished shopping, Kass dropped me back at home. Getting out of the house had brightened my mood; it had been exactly what I'd needed. I went upstairs to hang up my dress. The door downstairs shut and I raced back down, hoping it was Layna. I was so anxious for news on the hearing. Dalton hadn't texted or called me, and that made me nervous.

Layna stood in the hallway. I watched as she shrugged off her jacket and hung it on the coat rack, searching her face for any indication of what might have happened. Nothing. She looked up and saw me. A smile. A smile was good, right?

"How did it go?" I asked, my stomach in knots.

"Well," she smiled again. "He will be discharged from Tennerson's, but because you are not willing to make a complaint, we concluded that nothing could be proven, so this won't be on his record."

Yes! I ran up and wrapped my arms around her.

"Am I correct in that you won't be making a complaint?" she smirked.

I snorted and glowered at her. *Funny.* "Does he know?" I asked.

She nodded. "I just called him before I got in."

She'd barely finished speaking and I was back up the stairs, slamming the door to my room shut. I grabbed my phone and dialed his number.

"So you heard," he answered.

I threw myself on the bed and closed my eyes, focusing on his voice. I could almost imagine he was beside me, lying next to me. Touching me.

"I'm not going to lose my career."

"Yes, it's wonderful," I grinned into the phone. "I can't wait to see you."

"Me either. Come up to the city after graduation. Come stay with me."

"And your mom?" I piped up, cringing at the thought. I could only imagine what she thought of me. I was the girl who had stolen her little boy's heart.

"Mom can't wait to meet you, Wrenn," he chuckled. "Do you know how long she's been waiting for me to bring a girl home? I think secretly she always wanted a daughter."

"Even a student?" I joked feebly. "Okay. I'll come," I decided. At the very least, talking to his mom was probably what I needed to do most to make a decision on what I wanted.

"Good. I'm sorry I can't be there to see you tomorrow," he said, the disappointment in his voice obvious.

My mood dropped as I thought about how hard the next day

was going to be. I'd have Layna and Dan there, but my graduation was one of those things I'd expected to share with my parents and my brother. Not having Dalton there to see me graduate was just another blow.

"Don't worry, Layna will take plenty of photos."

"Good. I guess I'll see you soon," he said, his tone soft.

"Can't wait," I smiled.

***

Kass was over at nine in the morning to help me get ready. Personally, I didn't see the point in getting up so damn early when we didn't need to be at the auditorium until twelve, but I gave in. Who was I to spoil the sudden urge she'd developed to be all girly together?

"Are you going down tonight to see him?" she asked, running the straightener through her hair.

I nodded. At first I was going to stay \, then drive down the next day, go out for dinner with Layna and Dan and celebrate my graduation. Then I had the realization that the only person who I wanted to celebrate with wasn't here.

He was the only person I really cared about sharing anything with. And what's more, it hit me that I hadn't had a single nightmare about the accident since the day we met.

It was at that moment I knew that no matter what, I couldn't give him up. You can't choose who you fall in love with, all you can do is be damn thankful you've found someone who understands you.

Nobody understood me like he did.

***

I sat in my chair in my gown and my cap, waiting for my name to be called.

Then it was. I stood up and walked up onto the stage to collect my diploma. It was such a bittersweet moment; every emotion was hurling through me, from happiness and relief right down to anger and sadness. This was a milestone in my life that my family should have been here to see, and I was angry that had been taken from me.

I imagined them, standing underneath the huge oak tree over by the gardens. Mom would be smiling and clapping like crazy while dad struggled to figure out how to operate the video camera. Jordan would be rolling his eyes and trying to help Dad, while trying to hide the fact that he was proud of his big sister.

I reached the podium where Layna stood, holding my diploma. I could see the tears in her eyes and I knew she was thinking the same thing: my family should be here. I wiped my eyes and smiled at her, unable to hold back the tears.

"They would be so proud of you. Just as Dan and I are," she whispered in my ear. She kissed my cheek and hugged me as the small crowd clapped. "Now go over to the fire drill area."

What the hell? I opened my mouth to question. She shook her head and grinned.

"No questions, Wrenn. For once in your life, just do as you're told."

I nodded and made my way off stage as the graduates began to gather with their families.

I looked out over the empty gardens, puzzled at what I was supposed to be seeing. I passed the seating area, and the path that headed to the student parking lot, still unsure of what the hell I was looking for. *Had they gotten me a new car?*

"Hello, you."

I turned around, my eyes widening in shock. *Dalton.*

What the hell was he doing here? He stood there watching, amused by my reaction. His mouth turned upwards into a smile as I ran forward and into his arms. God I had missed him. Our lips melted together, his hand cradling the base of my neck, leaving my skin tingling and my mouth wanting more.

"I couldn't miss seeing you graduate," he murmured softly,

kissing my nose, then my eyes, then my forehead. "I called Layna and we agreed I would stand over here, away from…well, everyone."

I wrapped my arms around his waist, my head resting against his chest, so glad he was there.

I glanced back over at the crowd around the podium, which was beginning to dissipate. I wouldn't be going to the dance that night. I wanted to spend every moment with *him*.

"Come over to the house," I said, pulling him in that direction.

He raised his eyebrow at me as if to say 'now?' I giggled and blushed as I nodded my head furiously.

He shook his head and laughed. "See, you can't keep away from me, Wrenn. You can barely last a day without me around." It was true. The few days had been hell without him. If that hadn't already made my decision up for me, then seeing him here today sure as hell had.

As we walked away, I spotted Paige staring at us from the other end of the gardens. I slowed to a stop, my heart beating furiously.

"Can you give me a moment?" I said to Dalton. *I needed to do this. I needed closure.*

"Sure," Dalton replied, taken aback. He glanced around and spotted Paige, his body tensing. "What are you doing?" he asked uncertainly, his hand gripping my arm.

"Something I should have done a long time ago," I murmured. As he let me go, I walked over to her. She eyed me coolly, her lip turned up as I approached her. If she felt bad or embarrassed about what she had done, she didn't show it.

"I want to ask you something," I said, looking her in the eye. All the hell she had put me though and it came down to this: me finally confronting her.

"What?" she sneered in disgust. Her chin rose, like even talking to me was below her. She flicked her blonde hair over her shoulder and waited.

"I want to know what your problem is. Why do you hate me so much? What did I ever do to you?"

Paige laughed and shook her head. "See, you never did get it. You come in here, the little niece of the headmistress, acting like you're so much better than everyone else with your perfect little life." She pursed her lips, her eyes narrowing in on me. "I don't need a reason to hate you, Wrenn. I just do."

I began to laugh. She stared at me like I was crazy. Maybe I was. For so long I had let her get under my skin, and now I couldn't give less of a shit about her. The response she had just given me confirmed what I already knew: she was a selfish little brat.

"Do you know why I came here?" I asked her. I didn't wait for an answer. "Because my entire family died in a car accident. I lost my mother, my father, and my brother, Paige. Do you think I asked for this? Do you think I wanted to invade your little world?" I asked, spreading my hands. "My perfect little life ended a long time ago."

Her mouth fell open as her blue eyes filled with shame. She actually looked sorry. I almost laughed. The bitch actually had the balls to feel *sorry* for me.

God, that made me want to slap her.

"My God, Wrenn, I didn't know—"

"Of course you didn't, Paige," I cut in. "You *never* gave me a chance. All you did was make my life hell, and the lives of others. Do you think any of this matters? In ten years, where will you be? Still judging people on the very little you know about them?"

She didn't respond. Instead, she dropped her gaze and waited for me to finish.

"Do me a favor and learn from this, because often what seems perfect really isn't." I turned and stalked off before she could reply, flipping my hair over my shoulder.

Damn, that felt good.

***

"Are you sure we're not going to be…interrupted?" Dalton mumbled, kissing my neck. I nodded. Layna and Dan would be tied up with school-related graduation things for at least the next two hours.

Then, we were having dinner. The four of us—something that made me completely anxious. Since the truth about us had come out, I hadn't had the pleasure of being in the same room as Dalton and my family, so I had no idea what to expect.

Up on my toes, I curled my arms around his neck, tilting his lips down to meet mine, loving the feel of his hand on the curve of my back. Reaching for his hand, I led him to the bed, curling up with his arms around me. I didn't need sex to feel close to him. Just having him next to me was enough.

***

Well, this was awkward.

Dalton, Dan, and I sat at the table as Layna carried over the roast that had been slow cooking all day. The table was full of fresh rolls, beans, roast vegetables, and other foods, the smell of which were making my mouth water.

We sat in silence. And not the good kind, either. It was that weird, eerie silence where you rack your brain trying to think of some amazing conversation starter. I came up with nothing. I glanced at Dalton, silently willing him to say something. He shrugged helplessly.

Fuck.

"So, I'm finally free." It was the first thing that popped into my head. "No more school work. Not until college starts, anyway," I added. Okay, now I was just rambling, but it was better than the alternative.

"How does it feel?" asked Dan, relieved a topic had been put forward.

"Good. Kind of scary, but a good kind of scary." I felt Dalton squeeze my knee under the table. I put my hand on top of his and smiled at him, tensing as his hand wandered further up my thigh. My body tingled, his touch arousing me even in the presence of my family. I shot him a look. He winked at me, hiding a smile.

"So Boston University here you come, huh?" Dalton grinned at me, his hand still stroking my thigh.

"And how about you, Dalton? What are your plans now that the school year is over?" Dan asked pointedly.

Dalton glanced at me. "Well, Wrenn doesn't know this yet,

but I've applied and been accepted into study elementary teaching at BU."

I turned to him and gaped. *What?* He would be at BU with me?

"Really?" I squealed. I leaned over and kissed him on the cheek, throwing my arms around him. "Congratulations."

"Thanks," he mumbled, flashing me a smile. "I know we haven't talked much about the future, and I wouldn't accept the offer without talking to you first, but this is something I really want to do."

"I think it sounds perfect for you. And we would be in college together," I laughed. "How freaking weird would that be?"

"We would almost be a normal couple," he chuckled.

Layna sat down as Dan carved the roast. She smiled at Dalton, and I could tell she was genuinely happy for him. "That's great news, Dalton."

The rest of dinner went okay. It wasn't a completely natural, easy meal, but it was much less painful than I'd been anticipating. I couldn't expect for them to be comfortable with the idea of us being together right away, but the fact that they were trying meant the world to me.

***

"That didn't go too badly," Dalton chuckled, sitting down on my bed. "Are you sure it's okay for me to stay in your room?"

I rolled my eyes. "Yes, it's fine. I'm eighteen, remember? Hell, I'm not even in high school anymore," I joked. I walked over to the bed and joined him, lying on my side, my hand propped up against my head.

"And I'm glad," he grunted, shaking his head. "Believe it or not, you being my student wasn't a big turn-on—more like something I had to push out of my head."

I giggled. "Oh really? I thought that was every guy's fantasy. That and a three-way."

"The three-way, maybe," he laughed. "But seriously, I feel so much more comfortable about us now that school is finished. Though I think to everyone, I'm always going to be that creepy History teacher who took advantage of his student."

I smiled, rolling over so I sat on top of him.

"See, the way I remember it, *I* hit on *you*. In fact, I made every advance. You were the poor innocent teacher who was led astray by his pretty, irresistible student." I leaned down to kiss him.

He laughed and pushed me away. "No, I can't kiss you when you're talking like that," he chuckled. "But you are right about one thing: you are very irresistible."

We lay in bed with the TV on, watching horror movies for half the night. A few times I dozed off, only to wake up to him stroking my hair and smiling down at me.

"You've slept through most of this," he chuckled, kissing my nose.

"Big day," I mumbled, rolling over and falling back asleep.

Chapter Thirty-One

Wrenn

I'd never been to Los Angeles before.

It was pretty much as I'd expected: lots of traffic, people, and noise. Dalton snuck glances at me as we drove down the M1 heading toward Lanyard, where his mother lived.

We'd be staying with her for a few weeks, and then moving on to Boston where we planned to get a place together, ready for the start of university.

I was nervous about meeting his mom. She would've known my mom, and that connection gave me some relief. It was like we were all intertwined in each other's lives, and it was inevitable that we would one day meet.

Dalton's mom lived in a huge two-story brick house that overlooked Potter's Lake. The gardens were perfectly manicured, and the place was nicely kept. My heart was pounding as he pulled into the driveway.

What if she didn't like me? What if she thought I wasn't good enough for her son? As if sensing my concerns, Dalton gave me a smile, putting his hand on my thigh.

"She will love you, just like I do."

I turned to him. Though he had made his feelings clear, that was the first time he had told me he loved me. I brought his hand up to my mouth and kissed his fingers. "I love you too. So fucking much," I said, my eyes brimming with unwanted tears.

He chuckled and reached over to me, wiping them away. "Don't cry. This is a happy moment. Enjoy it." He smiled at me again. "I love you, Wrenn." He kissed me tenderly, his fingers brushing wisps of hair away from my face.

He was right. I deserved to enjoy this. Him. Everything. This was my happy ending. No matter what the future held.

***

Mary, Dalton's mother, turned out to be a lovely woman who I instantly liked. She hugged me as if we were old friends and ushered us inside. She took us through to the kitchen and demanded we sit down while she made coffee.

"It's lovely to finally meet you, Wrenn. I've been hearing such wonderful things about you."

I smiled. Who had been talking about me—Dalton or Layna?

"It's great to meet you too," I said earnestly.

She set a mug of hot coffee in front of me, and then Dalton. When she looked at him, I could feel the love. It almost took over the room. He was her baby and she would do anything to protect him. Only there were some things he couldn't be sheltered against.

"Did you make the appointment?" he asked her, fingering the handle of his mug. He looked up and waited for her to answer.

She nodded, biting her lip, her face giving away her anxiety.

"Thanks, Mom. It'll be fine," he assured her. "I'll be fine. No matter what, I'm okay. You don't need to worry about me."

She laughed, tears welling in her eyes. "Honey, I'm your mom. I'll always worry about you. It's my job."

***

It was after dinner, and Dalton had gone out to meet up with some friends. He had wanted me to go, but I'd claimed I had a headache. At first he'd wanted to stay, but after five minutes of me insisting he go out and enjoy himself, he relented. After he'd gone, I crept out of the guestroom, making my way to the living area, where Mary was reading. She smiled at me as I entered, putting down her book.

"How's your headache, honey?" she asked, her brow creased with concern.

"Better," I said, a wave of guilt washing over me. There had been no headache. I just needed an excuse to spend time with Mary. There was so much I wanted to know.

"Can I get you anything? A soda? A tea?"

I shook my head, curling up in one of the armchairs, my legs under me. I had no idea of how to broach the subject of the disease.

"Would you like to chat?" she asked gently.

I smiled and nodded.

She sat down in the chair next to me. "You're a strong girl, Wrenn. I know this feels overwhelming, but cherish the time you do have with him."

"What was it like? Watching your husband suffer?" That was the thing most on my mind, and something only she could answer.

"Awful. It was hard. And as bad as it was for me, I know it was worse for him." She took a deep breath, and then sighed. "Losing Derek was horrible, but I am thankful for the wonderful years we had together."

"Did he suffer?" I asked softly.

"The last few months were hard for him. I'm sure he was suffering, but by then he had trouble communicating…" Her voice trailed off as tears filled her eyes. I felt bad for bringing it up. "You can't control who you love, Wrenn and I think you know that better than anyone. If I'd known about Derek's illness, it wouldn't have changed anything. My love for him wouldn't have disappeared. The only thing that might have changed was that we wouldn't have had Dalton."

The power of her words hit me. Out of the tragedy of her husband's disease Dalton was born, and had she known about it, they wouldn't have risked having him. You can't live life waiting for things to go wrong, because then you're not really living. Everyone is going to die. That is part of the journey of living. What matters most is living each day you do have like it might be your last.

I stood up and hugged Mary, glad for her support, and knowledge. Whatever tomorrow bought, I was determined to be there for him. Because even just one day with him would be worth it.

Chapter Thirty-Two

Dalton

The test was a simple DNA blood test. My blood was sent to a lab where it was analyzed to determine whether I carried the disease. If I did carry it, then there was no doubt that I would develop it.

"What does this even mean?" Wrenn muttered, throwing the brochure back onto the side table. We were sitting in the waiting room of the doctor's office. I leaned forward and picked it up, sensing her frustration. She was nervous. We both were. I was shitting myself.

"The genetics of the disease are pretty complicated. Basically the disease is a genetic malfunction in the brain. It's the same message getting repeated over and over and not getting through to the parts of the body that need it. See here?" I pointed to the reference of the *CAG* genetic mutation. She nodded. "So if this repeats less than thirty-five times, then it's all good. If it repeats more than forty times, then not so good. The higher the number of repeats, the earlier the disease will develop."

"And it's usually worse with each generation?" she asked.

I nodded. "Not always, but usually."

Wrenn studied the brochure. "What if this gene repeats, say thirty-six times?" she asked suddenly.

"If it's less than thirty-nine, but higher than thirty-four, it's likely the disease will develop. I think its something like a seventy percent chance I'll show symptoms by the time I'm seventy."

"So even after all of this, there is a chance you won't have a conclusive answer?" she demanded.

I nodded.

"Then what's the point? Why are you doing all this if there is a chance it won't give you the answers you want?"

"Because no matter how small, if there is a chance I don't have this, that I'll never have this, I want to know about it. I want you to know about it." I sighed. This was so fucking hard. I struggled to think of what to say to her. How could I make her understand?

How could I put into words what I was feeling?

"Not knowing might as well be the same as knowing that I have this. It's always there, Wrenn. All these *what ifs* in the back of my mind, they don't go away. I don't want you to have to live that life too. If you're in this, then great, but you're at least going to know what it is exactly you're in for."

"I've already told you I'm in," she said with a frown, reaching for my hand.

"And I've told you that any decision you make before we know for sure, I won't accept," I said pointedly.

She rolled her eyes at me.

"It's a big decision, Wrenn. If I have this, I can't change that. But you have a choice. I never want you to feel like you don't have a choice."

"Dalton Reid?"

I looked up. The doctor stood in the hallway outside his consulting room. I nodded and stood, Wrenn rising with me. She clutched my hand tightly. She was shaking. I tried to give her a reassuring smile, but it came out more like a grimace.

We followed him into his office. I studied his face, looking for answers but he was giving nothing away. He would make an awesome poker player.

We sat down, waiting for him to take his place behind his desk. He nodded at me, raising his eyebrows at Wrenn. It had been years—about ten to be exact—since I had seen Dr. Martin. He hadn't changed much. His hair was grayer, and he looked older, but that was it.

"Dalton. It's been, what, ten years? You've certainly grown into a fine young man. I presume this pretty thing is your girlfriend?"

I nodded and chuckled as Wrenn's eyebrow shot up at being referred to as a 'pretty young thing.'

"This is my girlfriend, Wrenn." *Girlfriend. Wow, that sounds good.*

"Well it's lovely to meet you, Wrenn. I only wish it were under better circumstances."

My whole body tensed as he turned back to me. I studied his face. His eyes wouldn't quite meet mine and he kept wetting his lips, as though the air was sucking the moisture out of them.

This was bad. Oh God, I'm not ready to hear this.

"I'm sorry, Dalton. There is no easy way to tell you this, so I'm not going to beat around the bush. You tested positive. Forty-two repeats. You have Huntington's Disease."

That single moment I will remember forever.

My beating heart, the sound of my breathing, the ticking of the clock that hung on the wall. I was aware of Wrenn's stare, but I couldn't bring myself to look at her.

Positive.

Positive.

No matter how much you prepare yourself for hearing those words, there is always the tiniest part of you clinging to the hope that it won't be positive. All the times I had considered the disease, I'd never really believed that I would have it too.

I had Huntington's.

The disease that killed my father was going to kill me too. Well, that wasn't entirely true; dad had died from pneumonia, a complication of the disease, but *this* was my future. I felt frozen, unable to react. God knows what was going though Wrenn's mind. Maybe it would be best if she moved on without me. I had no idea what was next. What kind of life could I offer her?

"So, what now?" I asked, clearing my throat.

"Now, we monitor you. At the moment, every few years, we will follow up. Once symptoms develop, we will track the progression. This doesn't have to be a death sentence, Dalton. You probably have a good fifteen to twenty years before you develop symptoms. The CAG repeats are on the lower side of positive, and this is a good thing."

I wanted to laugh. Not a death sentence?

Says the guy who was *not* suffering from an incurable terminal disease that would slowly rob him of his independence, and eventually his life. I stood up, suddenly feeling claustrophobic, like the walls were closing in on me.

I need to get out of here. I felt sick. I headed for the door, knocking over my chair, with getting out of there the only thing on my mind. I made it outside, with no recollection of going through the waiting room area to get there.

Breathing in the freezing air, I gripped my hands behind my head, terrified and unsure of what to do next. Crouching down against the brick wall of the office, I slid down until I was sitting on the ground, my head in my hands.

"Dalton."

I felt her arms around me. I didn't look up. I couldn't. I couldn't stand to see her face. I didn't want to know what she was thinking. I didn't want to imagine living without her, or dying and leaving her.

"I can't do this, Wrenn. I can't just wait to die," I said, my voice breaking.

"Then don't. Live because you *can*. Live because you have twenty—maybe more—years before you show symptoms, then maybe another twenty. Live because you love me, and I can't stand the thought of losing you yet." She was crying, her dark hair enveloping my face, her soft hands warm against my neck.

God, I can't stand the thought of losing you either.

Chapter Thirty-Three

Wrenn

"I just want you to be sure."

I shook my head and laughed. How many times did I have to tell him that he was what I wanted? Many, it seemed.

"It's been a month, Dalton. Trust me, I've had time to settle. I've had more than enough time to think about things, and I have no doubt in the world that I want to be with you."

"Well, that's the best news I've heard all month." He smiled and cupped my chin, smothering me with sweet kisses. I closed my eyes and relished in the attention, loving every minute of it.

For the last few weeks we'd been staying with his mom. Dan and Layna had been down a few times, especially in the early days of his diagnosis. Those first few days were hell: everyone was acting like he'd died, mourning for the loss that might still be thirty years away. Things had settled down now, and were almost back to a normal routine.

The next week, we were moving to Boston. We had finalized the lease agreement on a little two-bedroom apartment not far from the university. I couldn't wait. Dalton was looking forward to his course, and because mine wouldn't start until next year I was going to look for a job. It was exciting planning a future with the man I loved.

I tried not to think about the diagnosis, because I was determined not to spend my time grieving. I'd done enough of that already.

***

I looked up from the jobs section of the *Boston Local* and saw Dalton's smiling face.

"For God's sake, Wrenn, enjoy your time off. Worry about work when we get there." He slid into the seat beside me, reaching for an apple from the fruit bowl in the center of the table.

I made a face at him. "Excuse me, but I want a job. I'm excited about getting out there and working."

"That'll last about a week," he chuckled.

I stuck my tongue out at him.

"Just because you have a poor work ethic doesn't mean we all have to," I said lightly, standing up and slapping him with the newspaper.

He caught my arm as I went to walk past and twirled me around until I fell into his lap. "You're lucky you're so beautiful," he murmured, kissing my neck.

I giggled as he worked his way to my lips. I would never tire of kissing him.

"You're fucking amazing, Wrenn, you know that? Not a moment goes by where I don't appreciate how lucky I am to have found you."

I smiled, wrapping my arms around him, knowing that I was the lucky one.

"I love you," I murmured, my mouth finding his. He kissed me roughly, his hands moving all over me, like he couldn't get enough. "I love you so much."

"God, Wrenn, I love you too." He shook his head and looked deep into my eyes. "Whether you realized it or not, since that first time we met all those years ago, you've inspired me to be more than I thought I ever could be. It was always you..."

THE END

Epilogue

Wrenn

Five years have passed since I graduated from Tennerson's. Dalton and I are still together, still very much in love. He shows no sign of the disease, and some days I see how healthy and strong he is and think they have to have made a mistake. He can't possibly be sick.

I'm in my final year of law school, and Dalton teaches at a local elementary school in Boston. He says his third grade students are much easier to handle than teenage girls, and I agree with him.

I'm getting toward that age where I think about having children of my own—then I wonder is it selfish of me to want that. I dread the day this disease takes hold of Dalton. Is it fair to put our children through that? I can't even imagine how hard it must have been for him, watching his father deteriorate; and as a mother, you'd want to protect them from that, right?

Even if it means not bringing them into this world?

Then I think about what an amazing man he is, and how lucky our children would be to have even just a few years with him.

I never thought that at twenty-three, these would be decisions I'd have to make sooner rather than later. Not once have I regretted my decision to be with Dalton. Everyday I feel his love for me and think how lucky I am to have found that.

I will make the most of the time I have with him, and together we will deal with whatever life throws at us.

Dalton

Every moment I spend with Wrenn is a gift, and one I am grateful for. So many people never experience love, and I'm lucky to have found someone I want to spend the rest of my life with.

I'm symptom-free and happy, and I try my damn best to appreciate that. I won't sit here and say it hasn't been hard. I wonder what is around the corner, and how we will deal with that.

You try to focus on the good, and for the most part you can do that. Then every now and then the negativity creeps in and you can't help but think about what you're going to be leaving behind.

I look at Wrenn and I see this incredible woman with such inner strength that every day, she amazes me. I want to give her the children she craves so badly, but I worry. Seeing my dad go through the final stages of this was hell—something I'd never want to inflict on another human being, let alone my own children. But is it fair of me to deny Wrenn the gift of being a mother? Because she would make a fucking amazing one. I don't know what the answer is.

For now, I'll continue to live my life and be thankful for what I have. There are so many worse off than me. I could have an aggressive cancer, or lose my life in an accident. We know what is coming, and no, it's not an easy thing to live with, but we still have today, and the next day, and the day after that.

Before I met Wrenn and when Dad was still alive, I remember sitting with him, watching him struggle to breathe and thinking to myself if it ever came to this I would end my life. I wouldn't let my family suffer the pain of watching me die. Now? I don't think I could do it. I couldn't rob her of those few precious extra moments together.

This disease sucks, but I refuse to let it define me. I'm determined to fill our lives with such happy memories that after I'm gone, Wrenn remembers only the wonderful moments we shared. Every day I make sure she knows how much she means to me. If there is one thing I've learned, it's that you can never tell someone enough how much they mean to you, because you never know when the day is going to be your last.

"*Live each day like there is no tomorrow, but don't forget to live each day like there was no yesterday either. Live in the present, for it is a gift from God. That's why it is called the present.*"—*Emily Austen.*

Looking for your next read? Check over the page for some great reccommendations.

Synopsis and excerpt for Very Bad Things, by Ilsa Madden-Mills

Very Bad Things, the #1 New Adult Romance from bestselling author Ilsa Madden-Mills.

"Very Bad Things is maddening, passionate, heart-breaking, all-encompassing, and about a million other adjectives." Books to Breathe

Synopsis:

Born into a life of privilege and secrets, Nora Blakely has everything any nineteen-year-old girl could desire. She's an accomplished pianist, a Texas beauty queen, and on her way to Princeton after high school. She's perfect…

Leaving behind her million dollar mansion and Jimmy Choos, she becomes a girl hell-bent on pushing the limits with alcohol, drugs, and meaningless sex.

Then she meets her soulmate. But he doesn't want her.

When it comes to girls, twenty-five-year old Leo Tate has one rule: never fall in love. His gym and his brother are all he cares about until he meets Nora. He resists the pull of their attraction, hung up on their six year age difference.

As they struggle to stay away from each other, secrets will be revealed, tempers will flare, and hearts will be broken.

Welcome to Briarcrest Academy…where sometimes, the best things in life are Very Bad Things.

Excerpt-

I purposely walked outside to the patio and strolled by his table, shooting him and his companions a flirtatious smile while he glared back. Then I went to the bar and ordered a glass of water. And waited.

It took fifty-three seconds for him to appear beside me.

"Not drinking today?" he said in a low voice, sending delicious tingles all over my body. He settled himself beside me on a stool.

"No fake ID," I said, putting my hand on his inner thigh and caressing the taut muscles there. "You seem tense. Is there anything I can do to help you relax?" I asked, my lips curving up in invitation.

He stared at my stroking hand and swallowed but didn't move away. "I just came over to see how you're doing," he said with a face like stone, not giving anything away.

I scowled and pulled my hand back. "Why? Because you feel bad for the poor little rich girl with all the problems?"

He looked away from me.

I said, "Let's go in the bathroom and fuck."

He exhaled heavily and stood up from the stool.

"No?" I said, feeling ashamed for the words coming out of my mouth, yet completely powerless to stop them. "You know, one of my favorite books has this sizzling chapter where the main characters go to lunch together. And even though it's a first date, they end up fucking in a bathroom stall because they can't wait to get at each other. He just bends her over and gives it to her, hard and fast. I'd like to reenact that scene." I took a hasty sip of water and got my nerve up. "All we'd have to do is pick the biggest stall, and then you flip my dress up and take me from behind. Or I could get on my knees for you?"

He paled and pinched the bridge of his nose. "You don't want me, Nora. I'll fuck you and when I'm done, I'll leave you."

All the air was taken out of me and a searing pain squeezed my heart so hard I thought I might cry out. "Well, if not you, then someone else will do," I said, looking around the bar. "Who should I choose? There's the young guy over there in the corner with the power suit and buzz cut who's been trying to catch my eye since I sat down…although I think I see a wedding band on his finger. He's out, I suppose. Even I have standards. And, there's the fortyish-looking guy sitting across from me. He's been staring at my breasts." I smiled and waved at the gentleman in question, and he waved back, a hopeful look on his face. "Oh yeah, definitely interested."

I opened my purse, pulled out a pen and wrote my name and number on a bar napkin. I pushed it over to Leo. "Do me favor? Take this over to him and tell him what a great girl I am. How good I am. How you know I'm not really bad." I stared at Leo's crotch. "Maybe tell him how hard you get when I talk about fucking."

He pulled me off the stool so quick I didn't know what had happened until I was standing right next to him, both of our chests heaving and tempers flaring. His eyes flashed. "Go back to your table. No fucking today, Nora," he bit out.

I smiled and batted my lashes. "Tomorrow?"

He growled at me and I thrilled at the sound, imagining him doing it while he made love to me. See, here's the thing: this was a whole lot more than just wanting to do bad things. I couldn't blame this on meaningless sex. No, this was all about him. About Leo. He sparked this insatiable, urgent need in me, one that I hadn't quite wrapped my head around yet. I'd never felt more alive than when I was with him, even if we were antagonizing each other.

"Are you high?" he asked me, his eyes boring into mine.

I laughed. "God, no. This is all me," I said bitterly. "I don't need drugs to be a whore, Leo. I can do it all by myself."

Connect with Ilsa:

Amazon: http://amzn.to/1ed1rVN
Barnes & Noble: http://bit.ly/1bOyH2g
Ilsa's Goodreads page:
https://www.goodreads.com/author/show/7059622.Ilsa_Madden_Mills
Ilsa's website: http://www.ilsamaddenmills.com/
Twitter: @ilsamaddenmills
FB: https://www.facebook.com/authorilsamaddenmills

Excerpt from Kitchen Pomises, Riveside Novel #3 by Brooke Cumberland.

Chapter One Excerpt-

Drake walked in wrapped in only a towel. The toast I was bringing to my mouth suddenly dropped from my fingers as my eyes roamed over his perfectly toned body. My eyes followed down to his perfect V that went just below the towel.

"Breakfast in bed and a show? I'm one lucky gal," I teased, leaning back against the headboard enjoying the view.

"Someone sounds like they are feeling better." He smiled.

"Well, I for sure am now."

"Really? Well, perhaps I should take advantage of that." He grinned, slowly unwrapping the towel from around his waist. I smirked as I watched him tease me, putting on a show as he finally released the towel. I watched it fall to the ground. I let my eyes wander up and down his body—appreciating every single chiseled curve of muscle.

"It's not nice to tease," I reminded him. "You better put out or get out."

"Oh, I love it when you talk dirty," he quipped, laughing. "I can't decide if I love or hate your pregnancy hormones." He grinned. It was true—I had a love/hate relationship with them as well. On top of always wanting to sleep and eat, I also wanted sex—*all the time*. Not that Drake minded, but some days, I was all over the place. I felt like I had no control over them. They were beginning to drive me mad.

"Can you be a little late for work today?" I asked, placing the tray of food on the bedside table. I didn't take my eyes off him as I watched him walk over to the bed. "I'd hate for you to get into trouble." I grinned.

"I could probably weasel my way out of it with the boss."

"You are the boss."

"I know." And with that, he made his way on top of me, brushing the covers off. "I think I can spare a few minutes…" He pressed his lips across my jaw, slowly moving to my neck. He bit it gently, making a moan escape my mouth at his touch and eagerness. "…for you."

His hands slid up my sides, taking my shirt up with them. I arched my neck to the side, giving him better access as the sensations riveted through me.

I reached down, pressing him harder into me. I felt his hardness against me, making me desperate and needy for him.

The hormones made my body respond to him so much more—not that I didn't before—but it was magnified. It was intensified, and I felt desperate to have him.

"Screw the foreplay. I need to have you right now," I demanded, pushing his body harder against mine.

"Such a romantic, aren't you?" I could feel him smiling against my neck as he continued softly kissing.

"I mean it. I'm going to explode," I breathed out rapidly. Just his touch could undo me completely.

"Alright, hold on, baby." He lowered his body and in one swift motion, slid my panties down. I wasn't looking for romance right now. I needed him just as much as I needed to breathe.

I threw my shirt over my head and unclasped my bra. It was still weird seeing my body naked with the way it was changing so fast, but it was also a constant reminder of the love Drake and I shared.

Instead of pressing into me like I wanted him to, he tenderly laid kisses over my stomach and in between my breasts. He was torturing me. He knew it, too. I was practically grinding against him, yet he refused to give in.

"Baby, please," I moaned out desperately.

"I can't help it. You are just so beautiful. You have the most beautiful pregnant glow." He continued to lay kisses around my bump, slowly, taking his time.

"That's great," I huffed, cupping his face up to look at me. "I'm going to handcuff you to this bed and straddle you if you don't—"

He forced two fingers inside me before I could finish what I was saying. I moaned loudly at the surprise sensation, arching my hips up to greet his fingers.

"You're feisty when you're desperate." He laughed as he worked his fingers in and out of me, hitting the perfect spot over and over.

I ignored him and grabbed the bedrail behind me, arching my body up to him as I needed and wanted to feel him inside me.

"How badly do you need it, baby?" Drake whispered with a hint of humor in his voice.

"You know how badly," I snapped, unable to open my eyes. Still, I could hear the amusement in his tone. He enjoyed torturing me and secretly loved it.

"Say it," he demanded, pressing harder into me, twisting his wrist, and practically taking all the air out of my lungs. "Say what you need, baby."

"I need you! I need you inside, right now. God, I swear, I'll do anything," I pleaded, willing to do just about anything to get what I wanted from him.

"Anything for my sweet girl," he hummed, lowering his lips to where his fingers were. He sucked hard, leaving no time for me to retaliate. My back arched, enjoying the sensations that released inside of me. My body shivered with pleasure, unable to control my own breathing as I moaned out.

He lifted his head and covered my body with his. I watched as he licked his fingers, moaning out pleasurable sounds.

"Keep your hands up," he ordered. I continued hanging onto the bedrail, tightening my grip as he finally pushed himself into me. The feeling was overwhelming as I took him all in, finally feeling full and satisfied.

He leaned down and kissed me gently as he rocked his hips into me. His breathing quickened as the air blew over my lips. His mouth wandered to my ear, blowing and licking over my lobe, making it harder to leave my hands up. I wanted to dig my nails into him and drive him insane as much as he was doing to me. He lowered his hand and cupped my breast, squeezing gently. I screamed out his name, pushing my breast into his hand urgently, desperately needing the release.

He lowered his face and took it into his mouth, swirling his tongue around my peaked nipple. He grabbed one leg and placed it on top of his shoulder, allowing him to get deeper inside me. That was enough to set me off. I screamed out, not holding back as I greeted his hips with mine, soaking up every pleasurable second.

It wasn't long before Drake did the same, milking his own release as he grinded into me. He lay on top of me as we both tried to get ahold of our breathing, panting into each other.

"Well, if this wasn't the best morning I've ever had—breakfast in bed *and* sex all before my shower." I grinned. My legs felt like jelly as all my muscles were stretched and aching.

"Glad to be of service." His voice was filled with amusement. I've been like this for the past few months—needing sex on demand. I felt bad, as if I were using him, but I figured it wasn't much different from before I got pregnant.

"Must be horrible for you, always needing to fulfill my needs, and all." I stroked his back with my fingertips as he continued lying on top of me.

"It's not always easy being the boss. Sometimes I have to do the dirty work." I could feel his smile against my chest as we bantered.

"Oh, you poor thing. I almost feel sorry for you." I rolled my eyes.

He kissed me lightly on the lips before rolling off the bed. I just watched as he walked to the bathroom. I listened as the shower started and steam began filling the room.

"Come on, let's shower together." He smiled, holding his hand out for me.

"Definitely the best morning ever." I grinned, taking his hand in mind as I followed him in.

And it *was* the best shower ever.

Connect with Brooke:
www.facebook.com/brookecumberlandauthor
Twitter @blcumberland
www.brookecumberland.com

Synopsis and extract from Songbird, by Lisa Edwards

Every relationship changes you, some for the better, others can shatter your confidence and almost destroy you.
For the musically talented, twenty-four year old Tara O'Connell, her relationship with Stephen almost broke her, until Tara found the strength to leave.
Now she is on the road to discovering that it is never too late to pursue your dreams and follow your heart.
As Tara's self-belief grows, she meets two men she is instantly drawn to who will change her life forever.
Corporal Riley Hammond is a soldier in the Australian Military Special Forces. With his smiling sapphire blue eyes, Tara falls for him instantly. He is thoughtful and caring, and gives her the support and love she needs.
While Cole Michaels is the overconfident singer in a popular local band. His charisma, emerald green eyes, tattoos and piercing, have girls falling at his feet. But while Cole pushes Tara's buttons, he also pushes her to reach for the stars.
Both men couldn't be more polar opposites, but both offer Tara different qualities that she needs to fulfil her destiny.
As Tara continues her journey, she will discover fate can offer you more than one path. Her fate is in her own hands, and the choices she makes, will shape her life forever.

Excerpt:

I went into the bathroom; Riley was still sitting on one of the dining chairs with a towel wrapped around his hips.

"You look very tempting," he said with a sexy grin.

"Why thank you," I said and gave him a catwalk twirl. I was wearing a little halter neck top, A-line skirt and a frangipani hair clip I had bought in Fiji.

"You look very tempting too," I said, appraising his nearly naked body.

He gave me a sad smile. "I guess it's time for a shave," he said, holding his razor. Then he held the razor up to me. "Would you like to do the honours?"

I'd never shaved anyone before and was a little nervous, but Riley seemed perfectly okay with it so I decided to give it a try.

He pulled me onto his lap so I was facing him with my legs on either side. "Can you do it from here?" he asked with a twinkle in his eye.

Now I was even more nervous as I reached around for the shaving gel and lathered his face.

"Do you trust me?" I asked seriously, looking into his eyes.

"With my life," he replied. Then added, "And my heart."

I kissed him delicately on the lips between the shaving foam. "Tell me how hard to press," I said as I started tentatively moving the blade down one cheek.

Riley reached up and took my hand, guiding it so I could feel the correct pressure and angle.

"Just like this," he said quietly, but his eyes were telling me he was thinking of something else entirely. He guided a few more strokes until I got the feel of it and then he let me take over.

His hands were resting on my thighs as I continued carefully shaving his face, then ever so slowly he started running them up and down my thighs, getting higher and higher.

"You're distracting me," I scolded him teasingly. I exhaled heavily and bit my bottom lip, trying my hardest to concentrate.

"You're distracting me," he retorted just as teasingly, watching my mouth. "Let's see how well you perform under pressure shall we."

His hands continued caressing my thighs then they slid higher under my skirt, his fingers gently pressing into my hips as he pulled me closer into him. He ran his thumb over the silky fabric of my thong until he found the spot he was searching for, then gently started stroking me.

I took my eyes off his neck to look directly into his eyes. I was trying so hard to concentrate on the task at hand but it was becoming increasingly difficult.

"I'm nearly finished, just give me a minute," I breathed as the pressure of his thumb increased slightly. I closed my eyes for a moment and shifted my hips subconsciously, a soft moan escaping as I exhaled, before looking back at his face.

His eyes were glowing with passion and I could see his chest rising and falling more rapidly, as he tried to stay still.

"Are you finished?" he asked huskily.

I dropped the razor into the sink. "Finished."

"Good."

His free hand was in my hair holding me in place as his lips enthusiastically met mine. His tongue searched my mouth before pulling away slightly and lightly biting my bottom lip. His lips made their way over my jaw, down my neck to my shoulder and I dropped my head back and closed my eyes, finally able to relax.

I ran my hands through his still damp hair and over his smooth cheeks then down his chest. His body felt amazing, his lips on my neck and shoulders felt incredible. He ran the tip of his tongue up my neck to just below my ear, and then nipped my earlobe.

I sighed, partly for the sensation on my neck and ear, and partly for what my palms were caressing, his glorious body, every muscle clearly defined.

He slid his thumb inside my thong as it continued its onslaught before reaching down and opening his towel, then effortlessly lifted me and pulling my thong to one side, lowered me down onto him.

I moaned deeply at the sensation of him inside me as I wrapped my arms around his neck, then set the balls of my feet firmly on the floor to get my balance.

Riley's hands were on my hips as they started moving me back and forth setting the rhythm and depth. I kissed him passionately on the lips, our tongues seeking each other's out as our pace fastened and the intensity grew. I was breathing heavily as I sat back and rested one hand on Riley's knee for balance.

He groaned deeply through clenched teeth and growled, "Oh fuck babe..." as he gripped my hips more forcefully, every muscle in his arms and chest tensed as he moved me back and forth, his eyes locked with mine.

I couldn't hold on. I dug my nails into his knee as my body tensed and I cried out. His release soon followed, his eyes never leaving mine until he finally pulled me into him and rested his forehead against mine, our hearts still racing.

"God I love you," he said breathlessly.

I smiled and rubbed the tip of my nose against his. "I love you too."

Connect with Lisa:
Facebook page: https://www.facebook.com/lisa.edward.9231
Author page: https://www.facebook.com/AuthorLisaEdward
Goodreads: https://www.goodreads.com/LisaEdward
Amazon: http://amzn.com/B00GW24MK4

Printed in Great Britain
by Amazon.co.uk, Ltd.,
Marston Gate.